"You're not telling me how to run my investigation, are you, reporter lady?"

His tone had that edge again.

Caroline stopped walking and her hands flew to her hips before she realized she was taking up her fighting stance. "So is this how it is between us, Sam? I'm Caroline if I play the game your way, reporter lady if I have an opinion of my own? If I show any spunk, you knock me down a peg or two, make sure I stay in my place. If I'm frightened and defenseless, you kiss me."

He met her gaze. Cold and stony, but there was something else there, a mysterious quality to him that she couldn't read.

"I didn't kiss you because you were defenseless."

Dear Harlequin Intrigue Reader,

We've got an intoxicating lineup crackling with passion and peril that's guaranteed to lure you to Harlequin Intrigue this month!

Danger and desire abound in *As Darkness Fell*—the first of two installments in Joanna Wayne's HIDDEN PASSIONS: Full Moon Madness companion series. In this stark, seductive tale, a rugged detective will go to extreme lengths to safeguard a feisty reporter who is the object of a killer's obsession. Then temptation and terror go hand in hand in *Lone Rider Bodyguard* when Harper Allen launches her brand-new miniseries, MEN OF THE DOUBLE B RANCH.

Will revenge give way to sweet salvation in *Undercover Avenger* by Rita Herron? Find out in the ongoing NIGHTHAWK ISLAND series. If you're searching high and low for a thrilling romantic suspense tale that will also satisfy your craving for adventure— you'll be positively riveted by *Bounty Hunter Ransom* from Kara Lennox's CODE OF THE COBRA.

Just when you thought it was safe to sleep with the lights off…*Guardian of her Heart* by Linda O. Johnston— the latest offering in our BACHELORS AT LARGE promotion—will send shivers down your spine. And don't let down your guard quite yet. Lisa Childs caps off a month of spine-tingling suspense with a gripping thriller about a madman bent on revenge in *Bridal Reconnaissance*. You won't want to miss this unforgettable debut of our new DEAD BOLT promotion.

Here's hoping these smoldering Harlequin Intrigue novels will inspire some romantic dreams of your own this Valentine's Day!

Enjoy,

Denise O'Sullivan
Senior Editor
Harlequin Intrigue

AS DARKNESS FELL

JOANNA WAYNE

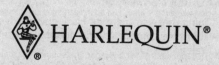

HARLEQUIN®

TORONTO • NEW YORK • LONDON
AMSTERDAM • PARIS • SYDNEY • HAMBURG
STOCKHOLM • ATHENS • TOKYO • MILAN • MADRID
PRAGUE • WARSAW • BUDAPEST • AUCKLAND

ISBN 0-373-22753-1

AS DARKNESS FELL

This edition published by arrangement with Harlequin Books S.A.

Visit us at www.eHarlequin.com

Printed in U.S.A.

ABOUT THE AUTHOR

Joanna Wayne lives with her husband just a few miles from steamy, exciting New Orleans, but her home is the perfect writer's hideaway. A lazy bayou, complete with graceful herons, colorful wood ducks and an occasional alligator, winds just below her back garden. When not creating tales of spine-tingling suspense and heartwarming romance, she enjoys reading, traveling, playing golf and spending time with family and friends.

Joanna believes that one of the special joys of writing is knowing that her stories have brought enjoyment to or somehow touched the lives of her readers. You can write Joanna at P.O. Box 2851, Harvey, LA 70059-2851.

Books by Joanna Wayne

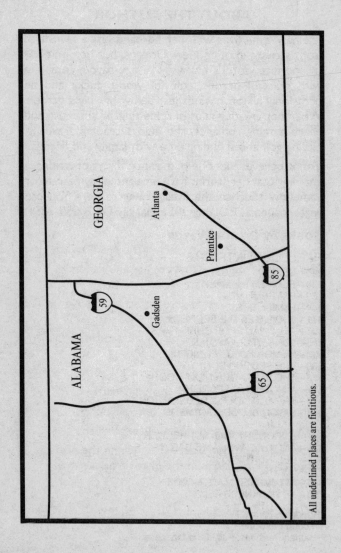

All underlined places are fictitious.

CAST OF CHARACTERS

Caroline Kimberly—She's a reporter trying to do her job, until the killer becomes obsessed with her.

Sam Turner—He's the detective in charge of locating the madman who's brought fear and murder to his peaceful Southern town, but will his attraction to the new reporter get in the way of his finding the killer?

Becky Simpson—Caroline's best friend, who only wants to enjoy the good life.

Jack Smith—Becky's new boyfriend.

Matt Hastings—Homicide detective and Sam's right-hand man.

John Rhodes—Editor in chief of the *Prentice Times*.

Ron Baker—Delivery coordinator and general handyman for the *Prentice Times*.

Tracy Mitchell—Works at the Catfish Shack and was a co-worker of the first victim.

Tony Sistrunk—Sam's former supervisor with the San Antonio Police Department.

R. J. Blocker—Sam's stepbrother.

Josephine Sterling—Police sketch artist.

Sally Martin—First victim of serial killer.

Ruby Givens—Second victim of serial killer.

Frederick Lee Billingham—The man in the portrait at the top of the stairs in the historic house that Caroline leases.

To my good friends Ted and Sylvia Ross whose romance
has withstood the test of time. And a special thanks
to them for being such great travel companions.

Prologue

"There is one thing I should tell you, Miss Kimberly, 'cause you're gonna hear it from the neighbors, anyway," Barkley Billingham said, examining her signature on the one-year lease she'd just signed. "My grandmother claims this house has ghosts."

Caroline looked at him, sure he was going to follow the statement with some kind of joke. But the guy just stared at her in the same deadpan way he had for the past two hours while she'd looked at the house.

"Why does she think the house is haunted?"

"You know how old houses are. They make noises. Creaks and moans, stuff like that. And when the north wind's blowing, it catches the corner by the bedroom and sounds like a woman shrieking."

"That's all?"

He folded the lease and tapped it against his arm. "Pretty much."

Caroline sighed. She could live with that, especially in a grand old house like this one. In fact, she couldn't imagine anyone with the kind of roots Barkley had here ever wanting to live anywhere else. "Are you the owner of the house?"

"No, it's still in my grandmother's name, but she moved to Florida. Lives in one of those places for retired folks. She thought the house was too much work. She talks about selling it all the time, but nobody wants to pay the kind of money she's asking for it."

"Did you move out because you think the house is haunted?"

"I'd have stayed. I was living free here, but I moved in with my girlfriend. I wouldn't worry none about the place being haunted if I was you. The house survived the Yanks coming down and destroying half of Georgia. Hell, I figure it can survive a few ghosts."

"Is that one of your relatives?" she asked, pointing to a painting on the wall at the top of a winding double staircase that could have come right from the set of *Gone with the Wind.*

"That's Frederick Lee Billingham, my great-great-great-grandfather. He's the one who built the house, and my grandmother claims he's hung in that very spot ever since the house was finished. She says he put a curse on the portrait, and if it's ever moved, Frederick will come back from the grave and woe unto the one who removed him from his place of honor. My grandmother is kind of nuts like that."

"Then I guess I better leave the picture hanging. I'm not looking for any woe."

"Suit yourself. You can do whatever you want with it. Same with this furniture up here. You can use it or stick it in the basement with the other old junk.''

"This isn't junk. I love the furniture up here, especially the sofa. I think the ghosts and I will get along just fine,'' she said, hoping she was right.

"Good. 'Cause they're all yours, as long as you pay the rent on time. How come you moved here to Prentice, anyway? Most people I know who are under the age of ninety are trying to get out.''

"I took a position with the *Prentice Times*.''

"What kind of position?''

"I'm a reporter.'' Well, she wasn't, but she would be, starting on Monday. She'd been a teacher in Atlanta until they'd let her go just two weeks before she was to start the year that would have given her tenure. But a job was a job, even one as a grunt reporter. And she loved the house.

"Don't see how they even sell those papers. Nothing ever goes on around here to write about, unless you're interested in that dumb historic pageant they do every summer in Cedar Park. Or the Heritage Ball.''

"I'm sure there'll be some news. They seemed eager to hire a reporter.''

She stood at the top of the landing as Barkley let himself out the front door, then turned to the unsmiling face of Frederick Lee Billingham.

"Glad to meet you, sir. I'll be living here now, and neither you nor any other Billingham ghosts are running me off.''

Actually, she couldn't leave even if she wanted to—not until next August. She had a one-year lease. And high hopes for a new life in the quiet, historic town of Prentice, Georgia.

Chapter One

Six months later

Caroline Kimberly swerved into the first available parking spot she saw, past the news van from the local TV channel and two police cars that showered the park and street with blinking red and blue lights. She grabbed her camera from the back seat, then scooted out from behind the wheel, slammed the door shut and cut across a grassy area. Big mistake, she decided as her high heels sank into the mud.

She jerked off her dangling earrings and stuffed them in her purse before she reached the cop standing guard over the gate. Unfortunately she couldn't do anything about the slinky red dress or the shoes. They'd been fine at her friend Becky Simpson's birthday party, but they were sorely out of place here. A jacket would be nice to cover her cleavage, but it was unseasonably warm for February and she didn't have one with her.

"Caroline Kimberly, the *Prentice Times*," she said, flashing her press ID.

The cop shone a beam of light at the card, then

looked her over, letting his gaze linger longer than necessary on the low-cut neckline of the dress. "If I were you, I'd go back to the party—unless you have a very strong stomach."

"What happened?"

"Somebody caught a touch of full-moon madness. Killed a young woman, cut her throat and gave her a bloody paint job."

"Full-moon madness?"

"That's what I call it. Something about the moon and the blood rush pushes crazies over the edge."

She shuddered and longed to turn around and go back to the party. But she'd worked hard to leave the ranks of grunt reporter and get a chance to cover some real news. Writing about murders had to be more challenging than covering a continuous run of ladies' auxiliary meetings and garden teas. Of course, she hadn't expected to run across a freshly butchered body her first week.

She scanned the area. No sign of her photographer even though he'd said he'd meet her here. Good thing she always kept her camera in her car. This could be big. She was glad her boss had gotten hold of the story so quickly, though it would have been nice if she'd beaten the TV reporters here.

"Get these people out of here—now. You can start with the broad on stilts."

Caroline spun around to see who was barking orders and singling her out for his scorn. The guy was tall and brawny, dressed in faded jeans and a black T-shirt that had seen a couple of thousand washings.

"I'm a reporter with the *Prentice Times* and I have every right to be here," she shot back.

"Wrong. It's a crime scene. You have no rights."

He stormed past her and headed to the spot where the TV camera was rolling.

"Obnoxious ass," she murmured, too low for him to hear, but apparently not low enough. Another cop stepped to her side while she stood there debating what to do next.

"Don't pay no attention to Sam," he said. "That's just his way."

"Rude and all bark?"

"Hell, no. Sam's more vicious than a bulldog on speed. I just meant you shouldn't take it personally. He feels that way 'bout all reporters."

That was just too bad. The TV cameras were running. She had to at least get a story. Someone else came up and started talking to the cop and she slipped away, this time all but running toward the action.

The cop yelled at her to come back. She ignored him, hoping that wasn't grounds for arrest. A few yards later she was close enough to see the body. The woman was lying on her back, naked. Her neck was gaping open and giant X's had been painted in blood across her breasts.

Caroline's stomach heaved and she turned away, suddenly so nauseated she could barely stand. Someone told her to get out of the way. This time she did, slinking into the nearby bushes and throwing up everything but the lining of her stomach. When she finished, the young cop who'd tried to stop her earlier was standing right behind her.

"Must have been something I ate," she said.

"Yeah. I almost did the same thing when I saw the victim."

Almost. Meaning he hadn't. She was obviously green, both literally and figuratively.

"Are you all right now?" he asked.

"I will be in a minute. What's the story on the dead woman?"

"There isn't one yet."

"Who found the body?"

"Not sure, but whoever it was called the TV station. They were here before the cops, which is why Sam's fit to be tied. Probably the most brutal crime to ever hit Prentice, and his crime scene is compromised."

"Is he in charge of the investigation?"

"He's the head of homicide. Makes sense he'd head up this one."

"What's his last name?"

"Turner."

Detective Sam Turner. The name seemed familiar, but she was certain she'd never met the man before. He might be irritating, but he wasn't the kind of man you'd forget. More intimidating than handsome, but rugged—and brawny enough that a woman had to notice.

"I hate to run you off," the cop said, "but Sam gave orders to clear the area of reporters."

Yeah, especially the "broad in stilts." She nodded and started back in the direction of the gate. Only, she made a turn at the last minute when she realized no one was watching her, took a deep breath to calm her stomach and rattled nerves, then walked back to the body. This time when she got there, she started snapping pictures, though she imagined they'd be too gory to run in the morning paper.

Detective Sam Turner appeared from nowhere and stuck his hand in front of her lens. "I hope there's a very good reason why you're still here."

"I'll be writing an article for tomorrow's edition of the local paper, and I have a couple of questions."

"Oh, well, let's just forget the killer and try to get you a story."

She ignored the sarcasm. "Do you have any suspects?"

"Hey, Turner," someone called from an area beyond the immediate crime scene. "Come take a look at this."

"Be right there." He turned back to her. "I don't have a suspect or a motive or even an identification of the victim, and I don't give a damn what you write in your little article. I do care that some woman was sliced up like a slab of meat, so if you'll get out of my way, I'd like to find out who did the carving."

"Should the public be concerned that..."

He turned and walked away as if she were a pesky fly not even worth swatting.

But he had told her what she needed to know. There were no leads and the victim was as yet unidentified. Slim, but she could stretch it into a front-page story, especially if any of the pictures were publishable.

This was no doubt the most macabre murder to hit quiet little Prentice in a long, long time. Maybe since forever. She'd have to call her boss the minute she got to the car and tell him to hold her a spot on the front page.

The *Prentice Times* was a small-town daily and John Rhodes, both editor in chief and managing editor, had a very hands-on management style. He'd want to see every word of this story before it went to print.

According to the lore of reporters, she should be experiencing some kind of rush right now. But all she felt was a queasiness deep in her gut and a nameless dread that seemed to reach clear to her soul.

She'd write the article, and every parent who picked up the morning paper would feel a knot of fear when they read it. Those who didn't know where their daughters were would become sick with worry.

This was some career she'd chosen—or that had chosen her. A frightening, challenging, dubious hell of a career.

COPS, TV CAMERAS, reporters. What a show. And down to a man—and woman—they'd recoiled at their first glimpse of the body. But they stayed and stared, soaking up the sight of gore as if they couldn't get enough.

They were wondering, no doubt, how it felt to actually wield the knife, imagining the frisson when the first blood spilled from her body. They envied him. Not that they'd ever admit it. They considered themselves above such cravings, but he knew better.

They were fascinated with the act of murder, the same way racing fans lived for the big crashes and people stayed glued to their TVs when tragedy hit.

He watched and studied them all, especially Detective Sam Turner. But his gaze was drawn again and again to the reporter in the sexy red dress. She was doing her job, but it was clear she was getting no respect. Sam Turner thought this was his game, but he was wrong. He'd find that out soon enough. They'd all find out.

Murder by murder by murder.

Chapter Two

It was ten minutes before midnight by the time Caroline had finished at the newspaper office and made it back to her house. As she'd expected, John was thrilled that she'd managed to get few pertinent details and a couple of usable pictures of the cops working the crime scene. He'd stood over her while she'd written the copy, making suggestions and asking questions, but when she'd finished, he'd told her what a great job she'd done.

She was tired, but the images from the murder scene stayed with her, replaying like a video in slow motion as she showered, brushed her teeth, then rummaged through her bureau drawer for something soft and satiny to sleep in. Lingerie was her one indulgence, a side effect of the years she'd had to wear nothing but functional cotton that could take lots of wear and harsh bleaches and detergents.

Tonight she slipped into a pair of pink silk pajamas with a matching robe. But even that didn't calm her mood. She went to the kitchen, poured a glass of wine and carried it with her as she roamed from one room to another. She loved the historic old house better all the time, even though the rent was a tad more than she could actually afford.

Sure the floors creaked and moaned and the ancient plumbing rattled, but the house had character and personality. It had seen weddings, births, countless celebrations—and deaths. It almost breathed stories of the past. So if a few spirits remained, who could blame them?

But she doubted any of the former inhabitants of the Billingham house had ever seen anything like the brutal murder she'd covered tonight. Caroline wrapped her arms around herself, suddenly cold and filled with a kind of nebulous apprehension, then climbed the creaking, winding staircase. The second-floor hallway was wide and high-ceilinged, and contained the furniture her landlord had left. A Queen Anne sofa so faded and stained, it was impossible to decipher the original color. An antique chest with spindly legs and broken pulls. A wavy wall mirror, bordered in tarnished silver, ornately embellished as if made for a queen.

And her favorite, a marred and stained secretary that had been made in France and shipped to America just before the Civil War. She'd found that out from records still stored in the secretary itself.

Caroline dropped onto the sofa and pulled her feet up beside her. Leaning back, she stared at the gold-framed portrait that hung above the staircase. Even at this angle, the eyes in the portrait seemed to be looking right at her.

"Things have changed, Frederick Lee. Time is no longer passing by your peaceful Southern town. History and modern macabre have now officially merged.''

Finally she gave in to the burning pressure of her eyelids and let them close. Her subconscious took over, forming new images out of gruesome reality. She was trying to close the victim's gaping wound while Detective Turner guided her shaking hand. They moved slowly and deliberately, as if working some deranged jigsaw puzzle. The pieces were there, but she couldn't make them fit. She was so tired. So very, very tired.

Slowly the images faded and she fell into the old nightmarish dream that had haunted her for as long as she could remember. The old church. The dark steep staircase. Dread so real she could taste it.

She jerked awake, the silk pajamas soaked with cold sweat that still beaded between her breasts and on her brow.

But it was only the nightmare that crept out from the dark recesses of her mind whenever she was stressed. Still, she flicked on the light. Frederick Lee was looking down on her, watching over her—at least, his painted eyes made her feel that he was.

It was nice to have him there.

CAROLINE STOOD with a dozen or more reporters at the news conference held at noon in Mayor Henry Glaxton's office. The room overflowed with eager reporters, but it became whisper quiet the second the mayor stepped behind the podium and adjusted the microphone.

He addressed the group in a smooth Southern drawl, expressing his condolences to the family of the victim, who'd now been identified as Sally Martin, and warning the citizens of Prentice to be cautious until the man who had committed the crime was identified and arrested. A task that he assured them was top priority.

The chief of police took the mike next. His explanation of the murder was brief. Sally had been a waitress at the Catfish Shack and was last seen alive at about 10:30 p.m. when she'd left work alone. Her car was found in the parking lot of her apartment complex, her handbag in the passenger seat, apparently untouched. There was no sign of a struggle. Like the mayor, the chief declined to answer questions. He'd leave that to the lead detective, Sam Turner.

"Which means we'll learn absolutely nothing," a reporter standing next to Caroline muttered. "Turner considers reporters disgusting parasites that exist merely to plague him."

Still, hands shot into the air as Sam joined the chief at the front of the room. He was no longer dressed in the faded jeans and T-shirt, but a pair of gray slacks and a light blue sports shirt, open at the neck. He cleaned up real good.

SAM LOOKED over the crowd and felt an annoying dryness in the back of his throat and a tightening of his muscles. As far as he was concerned, news conferences were a waste of time and a damn nuisance. He should be out in the field tracking down the murderer, not standing here trying to appease a bunch of clueless reporters.

"Do you think this was a crime of passion?"

"I don't stick labels on murders. I leave that to you guys."

"Do you think the killer knew the victim?"

"It's possible."

"Do you think this is connected to some kind of cult or devil worship?"

"We don't have any information to indicate that." Sam pointed at a skinny guy in the back of the room.

"If it's not some kind of cult murder, how do you account for the marking on the victim's chest?"

"I'm not jumping to conclusions and I'm not ruling out anything at this point."

"But you do think it could be some kind of ritualistic killing?"

"Anything's possible." How many ways was he going to have to say that before this was over? He glared at the waving hands, then pointed to the woman who'd thrown up in the bushes last night.

"Do you think the killer will kill again?"

Not the question he wanted. Not that he didn't know the answer. The guy was a walking time bomb armed with a hunting knife. And if Sam said that out loud, he'd send the town into total panic and give the mayor a heart attack.

"I think people should stay alert until this man's behind bars."

All the hands were flying now. He glanced at his watch. Five more minutes before he could cut and run. Five more minutes that the killer was walking free.

SAM TURNER was the first to leave the room when the conference was over. Caroline was the last. There was no reason for her to rush to the office and put a story together from the skimpy details that had been provided. The *Prentice Times* didn't run a Sunday edition.

She took the side exit, the one closest to her car. That side of the building was deserted, and for a second she had the weird feeling that someone was watching her. She turned and looked behind her. No one was there.

Still, she locked the car doors the second she got in, realizing that this was the first time she'd done that since she'd moved here from Atlanta. Instead of starting the engine, she took out her notebook and scribbled down her thoughts, not in reporter framework, but just in the order they flew into her mind.

A young woman had her throat slashed and blood smeared over her breasts. What would cause a person to do such a hideous thing? Anger? Passion gone berserk? Or had something in the killer's mind just slipped off center? And would he strike again?

Caroline's cell phone rang, startling her so that she jumped and bumped her elbow on the steering wheel. She checked the number. It was Becky. She took a deep, steadying breath before she answered, trying to dispel the dark mood that had come over her.

"Okay, I'm a louse," she said. "I should have called and explained my sudden departure just when the party was starting to get fun."

"No need. We figured you'd rushed off to a story. Was it the woman whose body was found in Freedom Park?"

"Yeah."

"I was afraid of that. That must have been totally gruesome."

"Pretty bad."

"We'll have a beer later. You can tell me all about it."

"You'll need more than a beer if I do."

"You sound upset."

"A little. Actually more than a little," Caroline admitted reluctantly.

"Maybe you should ask your boss to put you back in your old assignment."

"Just wimp out?"

"Hey, if it involves murder, I would," Becky said. "Anyway, I just wanted to make sure you were all right."

"Fine. How did the rest of the party go?"

"Not a lot happened after you left. We danced awhile. The party started breaking up about midnight."

"So how does it feel to be the ripe old age of twenty-six?"

"Not bad. I checked for new wrinkles this morning, but didn't find any. Of course, it could be that my eyes are going."

"No. I'm already twenty-seven, and I can still read the very small letters they print my name in when they bother to add it to my copy," Caroline said.

"Tell them to make it bigger or you'll quit."

"And who would pay my rent?"

"I'll lend you money. I have plenty."

Which was quite true. Not only were Becky's parents well-off, but her grandmother had left Becky a trust fund that ran somewhere in the millions. Caroline wasn't even sure Becky knew what she was worth. And not only was she rich, she was fun, petite and cute, with baby blue eyes and bouncy blond curls that danced about her tanned cheeks.

"I'll just keep working," Caroline said. "It keeps me out of trouble."

"It won't if you keep wearing that red dress you had on last night. You were hot!"

"Do you think it's appropriate for shopping at flea markets? That's about the only place I go these days, except for work."

Caroline stuck the key in the ignition as she talked, then noticed a yellow square of paper stuck under her windshield. Not a parking ticket, but some kind of note.

"Let me get back to you, Becky. I've got some business to take care of."

"Okay, but first, what did you think of Jack?"

"Do I know a Jack?"

"He was at the party last night. Cute guy. Blond hair. I saw you talking to him before he left."

"Oh, yeah. He seemed nice enough. Why?"

"I just wondered."

And probably wanted to fix her friend up with him. But the guy obviously wasn't interested, or he wouldn't have cut out early.

They said their goodbyes and she opened the door and retrieved the note. It was about three inches square with a sticky strip across the back. She might have spoken too soon about how acute her vision was. This time she had to squint to read the tiny, but very neat, print:

I saw you last night in the park. You look good in red. Come to my next party. I'll be looking for you.

She read the note again, but this time her blood ran cold. *My party.* Surely this couldn't be from the deranged bastard who'd killed and cut up the woman in the park. Yet...

She sat there, shaking, holding the note and staring at it until her fingers grew numb. Finally she turned the key and the engine purred to life. She yanked the car into gear, then waited for a black sedan to pass.

Driving the sedan was none other than Sam Turner, talking into a cell phone without even a glance her way. She pulled out quickly and stayed close behind him, not sure that following him was a smart thing, but thinking she should show him the note.

Two blocks later he pulled into the parking lot of the Prentice Bar and Grille. She lingered in the car, giving him time to go in and be seated while she pulled herself together. Her first murder assignment. And now the killer wanted her for a pen pal. It was the stuff of horror movies.

Once inside, it took her a minute or two to locate Sam. He was in a booth in the back, on his cell phone again, one hand cradling a tall glass of iced tea. He looked even more imposing here than he had at the crime scene and the press conference.

"Table for one?"

She smiled at the hostess. "I'm with the guy in

the back, the one wearing the blue shirt.'' She nodded in his direction.

"Sam didn't say he was expecting anyone."

"I wasn't sure I could make it." She brushed past the waitress, made her way to Sam's booth and slid in across from him.

He glared at her but finished his conversation. When he was through, he laid the phone on the table and made eye contact. His eyes were a deeper brown than his short hair, and she had the feeling he could see right through her. But mostly it was the sheer virility of the guy she noticed. He seemed to ooze testosterone.

"The news conference is over," he said, his tone commanding.

"I don't have a question. I have information."

His expression changed very little. "What kind of information?"

She pulled the note from the side pocket of her handbag and slid it across the table toward him. "I found this on the windshield of my car after the press conference. I think you should read it."

The condensation from his glass of tea had wet his fingers. He wiped them on a paper napkin and picked up the note, careful to touch only one corner. To avoid fingerprints, she was sure. Now why hadn't she thought of that?

He read it slowly, his expression unchanging. But when he looked up, his gaze was piercing. "Where were you parked?"

"Behind the administration building. Between Cork Avenue and Savannah Street."

"Did you see anyone when you approached the car?"

"No, but I had this strange feeling someone was watching me."

"A feeling?"

"You know, just an uneasy sensation. And I'm not usually a nervous person."

The waitress appeared and put a plate overflowing with a hamburger and fries in front of Sam. Caroline ordered a diet soda, quite certain it was all her stomach could handle at this point.

She waited until the waitress had walked out of hearing range before she asked the question that consumed her thoughts. "Do you think this note is from the man who killed Sally Martin?"

"It's hard to say. That's obviously what he wants you to think."

"But who else would write something like this?"

"Any time there's a murder like this, it brings out the weirdos."

"You talk as if you've seen a lot of murders like this one."

"I've seen my share. What about you, Miss…?"

"Kimberly, but you can call me Caroline." She hesitated, hating to admit the truth but seeing no reason to lie. "This is my first one."

His face remained unreadable. "Are you with a newspaper or a TV station?"

"The *Prentice Times*."

"I thought Doreen Guenther handled their crime beat. Not that Prentice had much of a crime beat before now."

"Her mother's ill. She took a family-emergency

leave.'' The waitress returned with Caroline's drink. She slipped the straw between her lips and took a huge sip, needing to soothe her dry throat. "So what do I do now?"

"I'll take the note and try to get some prints off it, but I doubt I can, since you mishandled it."

"I didn't know it might be from the killer when I tore it off the window."

"If you get another, I want you to lift it by one corner and put it in a plastic bag. And call me immediately." He took a business card from his shirt pocket and passed it across the table. "Use the cell number. And just for the record, I wouldn't publish the fact that the killer may have contacted you."

"Why not?"

"Whether the note's a prank or from the killer, publicity is likely to spur him on."

"So I may just keep getting these notes?"

"It's hard to say."

"Do you ever say anything definite?"

"When I have something definitive to say."

Yeah, well, she was beginning to wonder if he had a clue what he was doing or if he was just faking the whole experience bit. Which didn't make her feel any better, considering she was getting fan mail from a killer. "Why me?" she murmured more to herself than to Sam.

"You didn't exactly fade into the crowd in that getup you had on last night."

"I was at a party when my editor called and told me to head straight for Freedom Park. I didn't have time to change into something appropriate for a murder scene."

"No reason to get huffy with me. You asked why you were singled out. I was just answering." Sam slid his plate in front of him and switched his attention to the loaded sesame bun. She figured that was her invitation to leave.

She took another sip of her drink, then wiped her hands on her napkin. The man was too calm. If he thought she'd heard from the killer, he should be doing something. She wasn't sure what, but she wasn't a detective. "Aren't you going to ask for my phone number in case you think of something else to ask me?"

"Your number's easy enough to get."

"It's unlisted."

He took another bite of his burger.

She stood and slung her handbag over her shoulder.

"One more thing, Miss Kinnerty."

"Kimberly. Caroline Kimberly."

"Miss Kimberly, whoever killed Sally Martin is a very dangerous man. Don't try to be a hero."

"That, Detective Turner, is the farthest thing from my mind."

"Keep it that way."

And that was it. Not even a thank-you for coming to him with the information, though she knew there were some reporters who wouldn't have. They'd have played along with the killer in an effort to get a really big story.

Instead, she was playing with Sam Turner. She was certain it was not going to be a fun game.

SAM WATCHED Caroline walk away, a thousand memories tramping through his mind, none of them welcome. He wasn't sure what it was about the reporter that reminded him of Peg. They didn't look the same. Peg's hair had been long, whereas Caroline's was short, and the color of wheat, whereas Caroline's was more like café au lait.

But something about Caroline reminded him of Peg and that was enough reason to make sure he kept his distance from her. Something that might prove very difficult if she became his link with a killer.

He'd lost his taste for the burger, but he finished it, anyway. He ate from habit, the way he did a lot of things these days. Eat and sleep and breathe. Go through the motions.

Let it go, Sam, or it will eat you alive.

That had been the police psychiatrist's advice after Peg's death. Shows how little the shrink knew about him. Except for the motions, Sam was already dead. And there was no letting go.

IT WAS HER DAY OFF, so when Caroline left the Grille, she went home, glanced at the day's mail and made herself a salad that she barely touched. Nothing she did took the murder or the note off her mind. Finally she took a glass of chardonnay and climbed the stairs to the second floor to tackle cleaning the huge hall closet, a task she'd put off ever since moving in. But today the thought of escaping into someone else's old junk seemed more of a reprieve than work.

Thunder rumbled in the distance as she opened the closet door and breathed in the musty odor. No telling what skeletons might climb out when she started rummaging through the tattered boxes. The good thing was, they wouldn't bear any of her DNA. The bad thing was, neither did any other skeletons she knew anything about.

Wrapping her arms around a large box that sat on the closet floor, she tugged until it was out in the open. The tape that held it closed was brittle and peeling, and it took only a yank to loosen it.

The box was carefully packed, full of sealed plastic pouches. She opened one and pulled out the contents. Yards of teal satin spilled out. It took her a few seconds to realize it was a dress.

Standing, she held the dress to her shoulders to get the full effect. The full skirt hit just above her ankles, hiding most of her legs, but the neckline was plunging. A gown fit for a formal party in the late 1800s—or perhaps a madam in a fancy brothel.

The dress appeared in too good a condition to be authentic. More than likely it had been made for the annual spring pilgrimage event, when many of Prentice's historic homes opened their doors to the public. It was traditional for the hostesses to dress in the style of the period during which the houses had been built.

Caroline had first met Becky at one of the pilgrimages three years ago, her first year as a teacher. She'd brought a group of her students down to tour the houses and Becky had been one of the guides.

They'd hit it off from the moment they met, more because they were so different than because they were alike. The friendship had paid off in lots of ways. Becky was the one who'd told Caroline about the *Times* looking for a reporter back when she'd lost her teaching job.

Stripping off her slacks and sweater, Caroline

lifted the dress and fit her head inside the opening, letting the dress slide into place. The full skirt swirled about her legs as she danced over to the antique mirror and stared at her reflection. The distortion of the wavy glass was more pronounced than usual in the grayness of the cloudy afternoon, giving the shimmering dress a luminance that seemed almost magical.

The moment ended abruptly at the gong of the doorbell. She wasn't expecting anyone. But then, she hadn't been expecting a call to a murder scene last night or a note from a weirdo today, either.

Lifting the full skirt, she hurried down the winding staircase. The doorbell rang again before she got there, this time prolonged. She stopped at the door and looked through the peephole. Sam Turner.

And if he thought her outfit last night was a bit much, imagine how he'd react to this one. She started to yank the low-cut bosom up, then changed her mind and tugged it lower, leaving lots of exposed cleavage and little to the imagination. Might as well shock the detective all the way. Too bad she didn't have on her stilts.

She swung open the door and smiled up at him. "Hello, detective."

SAM ROCKED back on his heels, speechless. Whatever he'd expected, it wasn't this. "Am I interrupting something?"

"No, I'm just relaxing. Care for a mint julep on the veranda?"

He didn't answer, just worked to drag his gaze away from the pink mounds of flesh peeking out of her dress. Another fraction of an inch and her nipples would have been staring back at him.

"That was a joke, Detective. There's not a mint or a julep in the house. I was just cleaning out a closet, found the dress and tried it on."

"Good. I thought you might be expecting Rhett Butler."

"No. I hate men who don't give a damn." She opened the door a little wider. "Now that you're here, I guess you should come in."

"Just for a minute."

"Were you able to get prints from the note?"

"Only one set besides mine on the right edge."

"And the one set would have to be mine."

"It appears that way."

"I doubt you came all the way over here to tell me that."

"No. I have a proposition for you."

"I don't sleep with cops."

"Good, since I wasn't going to ask you to. I'd like you to take a run over to the crime scene with me."

"You want me to go to the park where Sally Martin was murdered?"

"That's right. It won't take long."

She took a step backward. "I'd rather not go back there, Detective."

Now that surprised him. Every reporter he'd ever known would have been salivating at the possibility of visiting the scene of the crime with the lead homicide detective. "It could be important, Caroline."

"Why?"

"I'd like you to show me exactly where you were at all times last night. Where you parked your car.

Which areas of the park you were in, that sort of thing.''

''I was only there a few minutes.''

''Long enough for the killer to see you, if in fact he was the one who wrote the note. You may have seen him, too, without realizing it. If we go back there, I can get a better feel for where he may have been standing while he was watching you. It might even trigger a memory of something you've forgotten.''

''I didn't talk to anyone except cops.''

''Look, I know this won't be as much fun as playing dress-up, but I have a dead woman, a brutal killer on the loose and no leads. Now are we going to stand here and quibble, or are you going with me?''

''Since you put it that way, I don't have a lot of choice. I'll need to change first.''

''A good idea.'' Hopefully into something that completely covered her breasts. ''Make it quick. The storm's blowing in fast.''

She turned and hurried away, leaving him standing by the door. Her skirt swished about her ankles, making soft, crinkly sounds that seem to slide under his skin.

What the hell was it about her that got to him like this? Or had it just been too damn long since he'd been with a woman?

Not that it mattered. He had a killer to catch.

A killer who had Caroline Kimberly on his mind. It was no time for Sam to be lusting after her, too.

Chapter Three

There was no bloody body waiting, but Caroline found the park even more ominous and cryptic than she had the night before. Dark clouds, heaving with moisture, rolled and tossed in the wind, and bolts of not-too-distant lightning were followed by rumbling claps of thunder, adding to the eerie feel.

A group of teenagers carrying skateboards stopped to watch them as she and Sam got out of the car. Her imagination flew into overtime and she tried to picture one of them wielding the knife and cutting Sally Martin's throat. But the innocence on their faces made them seem incapable of such brutality.

Sam glanced their way, then appeared to dismiss them as inconsequential. "It's going to pour soon, so let's get started."

"What do you want to know?"

"Where did you park your car last night?"

"Down the block, near that big oak." She pointed to a tree whose branches canopied the narrow neighborhood street.

He didn't bother to wait for her, just strode off in that direction, his gaze scanning the area. Once under the tree, he threw back his head and stared into the branches above him as if he expected the killer to be sitting there, waiting. "Was there anyone standing nearby when you got out of the car?" he asked when she finally caught up to him.

"There were clusters of onlookers everywhere, but I didn't notice anyone in particular."

"Did anyone speak to you?"

"Not then."

"You're sure?"

She tried to think back. Her mind had been on so many things when she arrived last night. Her photographer. The lights of the police cars and the TV cameras. Her inexperience in such a situation. Still, her memory was usually good for details. "I don't remember speaking to anyone until I reached the gate. I showed my ID to the cop who was standing guard, and he took one look at my dress and said I should go back to the party unless I had a strong stomach."

"So you marched right in?"

"It's my job." It still was, so she looked around, trying to take in as many details as she could. The park took up a full city block. There were baseball fields to the back, a jogging track, trees and walkways and a play area with picnic tables off to the right, near a wooded area. That was where the body had been.

Across the street from the park were small houses, mostly brick fronts with touches of stucco. A few had porches. A middle-aged man sat in a porch swing in the house directly across from them, watching them as he swayed back and forth. It was a natural thing for him to do, but still, his gaze made her uneasy.

"Do you think the killer was watching me even before I entered the park?"

"Possibly."

"From one of the houses?"

"He could have been watching from any number of spots. A house. Sitting in a parked car. Crouched behind someone's bushes. From the edge of the wooded area. But more likely he was just mingling in the crowd of bystanders."

And if the guy had been there last night, he could be out there somewhere now. She could all but see his eyes. They'd be dark, piercing, threatening. "Do we have to go inside the park?" she asked, anxious to get back in the car and drive away.

"It would help. Just retrace your steps, and I'll follow you."

They walked back to the gate as another bolt of lightning hit, this one way too close for comfort. Once inside the gate, she headed straight for the area where she'd first seen the body. "I started to follow the lights from the TV crew," she said. "That's when you spotted me and told some cop to order the broad on stilts out of here."

"Apparently it didn't do a lot of good."

"The cop told me to leave, but when he got side-tracked, I went back to my job. The public has a right to know."

"So you ignored police orders. Then what?"

"I looked at the body, and…" Damn, she hated to admit her weakness in front of this detective.

"You threw up in the bushes."

"How did you know that?"

"You were quite a hit last night. Wasn't a cop on duty who didn't notice the reporter in the red dress."

Cops. Killers. She'd impressed them all, except for Detective Sam Turner. He kicked a small pebble. It flew through the air, coming to a stop just inside the yellow police tape that circled the area where the body had been found.

Bloodstains were still visible, though they'd probably fade after the rain. But the images in Caroline's mind were still as clear as if Sally had still been lying in the grass. She shuddered and stepped away.

Sam took her arm. "Steady now. We'll be through here in a minute."

"Do you ever get desensitized to murder?" she asked.

"No. If I did, I'd get out of the business."

The admission made him seem more human somehow. It meant he wasn't all roar and rumble. Might even have a heart beneath that brawny chest. "Have you ever been on a case where the killer contacted someone he'd seen at the crime scene?"

"No, but it's not unheard of. I remember reading about one case on the West Coast a couple of years ago. Serial killer called a female news anchor before every crime."

"What happened?"

He shook his head. "I don't remember."

She didn't buy that for a second. "He killed the woman he'd called, didn't he?"

For the first time since they'd been in the park, he turned his attention totally to her. "Nothing will happen to you, Caroline. Not unless you let this man draw you into his sick games.''

The first drop of rain fell, quickly followed by others. They splattered on her nose and ran down her cheeks. Sam grabbed her hand and started running toward the car. But the storm's fury didn't wait. The rain blowing into her face stung like needles, making her contact lenses blur until she could barely see. By the time they reached the car, her clothes were soaked and water from her hair was dripping down the back of her neck.

Sam started the ignition and turned on the heater, but he sat for a minute before putting the car in gear. She had the feeling there was something else he wanted to say, but if there was, he changed his mind. He kept his gaze straight ahead as he pulled away from the curb.

Don't get drawn into this.

Good advice, only the killer had drawn her in the second he'd singled her out and delivered his note. With that one act he'd robbed her of any chance of the objectiveness reporters were supposed to maintain. Nonetheless, she'd keep things under control, report the news and do a good job of keeping the citizens of Prentice informed.

And pray he didn't contact her again.

''I TALKED TO every neighbor on the block,'' Matt said, scooting his notes in front of Sam. ''Everyone claims not to have seen anything until the television news van arrived.''

Sam picked up the notes the young detective had made, reared back in his chair and propped his feet on the desk. "Did you check to see if anyone in the immediate area has a record?"

"All the adults are clean as a whistle. One of the teenagers on the block has a battery charge against him."

"Details?"

"Gregg Sanders. Age seventeen—sixteen when the charges were filed. Attacked his stepfather with a baseball bat when he caught him fondling his little sister. Stepfather denied it. Kid got off with a warning, so I'm guessing the judge believed him, instead of the old man."

"Where's the stepfather now?"

"Out of the picture. Mother divorced him and has no idea where he's living, but is fairly sure he's not in Prentice."

"Any known sex offenders in the neighborhood?"

"None that showed up in the records."

"What about the search around the crime area?"

"We bagged some items. A couple of cigarette butts, an old sock, some chewed gum, a beer bottle, that kind of stuff."

"Send them to the crime lab in Atlanta. See if we can get a DNA reading from any of them."

"You got it. Anything else you need before I head out?"

Sam glanced at the clock. Five after five. Knock-off hour for the day shift. Time was when a cop on a murder case wouldn't have bothered to look at a clock. But those were guys from the old school. Today's cops had lives. They worked their shifts and that was it. They were probably better off for it. But then, so were the criminals.

"Guess that's it," Sam said. "Got a big night planned?"

"A hot date with a cute little redhead who works for Dr. Wolford. What about you?"

"I might cut out early and get some sleep."

They both knew he wouldn't. Sam would stop in at the Grille for the daily special, if he bothered to eat at all. After that he'd be back here at the precinct, going over the sketchy evidence.

Sam dropped the notes on the table as Matt left, then walked to the window and stared at the rain. It wasn't falling as hard as it had been when he and Caroline had been caught in it, but it was steady.

Caroline Kimberly. She should have no meaning to him at all except as she related to the murder case. Only now, standing here staring at the rain and thinking about how she looked soaked to the skin, he knew she affected him in ways he couldn't begin to define.

Not simple, like plain old-fashioned lust, though there was no denying he'd felt a tightening in his groin when she'd opened the door this afternoon.

But it had been even worse driving her home from the park, and she'd looked a little like a drenched, stringy-haired waif at that point.

Frustrated by the needs pushing at him from all directions, he crossed the room, opened his desk and pulled out the framed picture of Peg. He used to keep it on top of his desk, but he got tired of answering questions about who she was. So he kept it here for special times, when he needed to remember what life was supposed to be like. What it would have been like now if he hadn't made that one fatal mistake and let a killer sneak into their lives.

The kind of mistake Sally Martin must have made. Had she trusted a stranger? Prentice was the kind of town where that could easily happen. An hour southwest of Atlanta, but a world away from big-city problems. More churches than bars. Clean streets. Landscaped lawns. Citizens who still held to the old Southern ways and treasured their past as if it were a gem to be polished and put on display.

Had the killer merely left the interstate and driven the twelve miles along the state highway, winding up in Prentice with the urge to kill tearing at his soul? Or was it someone Sally knew and trusted? A betrayed lover?

But if there had been a lover, the Martin family had never heard of him. Their story was that Sally had flunked out of Auburn University last semester and had come home to get her act together before returning to school. Now she was dead.

Sam had no reason not to believe the parents. Their grief seemed heartbreakingly genuine. Besides, Sam's gut feeling was that the killer had picked Sally randomly or from some search criteria only he understood. He'd stripped her naked, but there were no signs of sexual assault.

Still, Sam was fairly sure the perp was male. The MO wasn't that of a woman. The knife, the nudity, even the marks on the breasts all indicated that the killer was a guy, either one strong enough to overcome the victim or charming enough to have convinced her to go with him willingly.

And unless Sam had this all wrong, the guy wasn't

through with Prentice yet. Nor was he through with Caroline. Sam had no evidence to support that or even to prove that the note left on the reporter's window was from the killer. It was all instinct. The stock and trade of any homicide detective worth his paycheck.

His mind went back to Caroline Kimberly. He'd done some checking on her this afternoon. She was new at reporting. New to Prentice, as well. Could she be…?

No. No way was she in this with the killer. And he doubted seriously she'd faked that note just to draw more attention to her reporting. Still, it never hurt to check out all the angles.

After all, his instincts weren't infallible. Peg's death was proof of that. He walked back to the desk and made a note to himself to call Sylvia in records tomorrow and have her run a more thorough check on Caroline Kimberly.

BY WEDNESDAY AFTERNOON Caroline had run out of things to write about Sally Martin's murder, but the town had not run out of their avid fascination for details. She didn't know if it was due more to their fear or their curiosity for the morbid, but the *Prentice Times* was selling twice as many papers as usual.

John was pleased with her work, but he kept pushing her for more articles. He wanted interviews with Sally's neighbors, her family, the people she worked with, even her high-school friends. It was almost to the point where anyone who'd ever passed Sally Martin on the street could get his or her name and opinions in print.

"I'm making a Starbucks run," Dottie said, walking through the office with pen and notebook in hand. "Who wants what?"

Dottie was their teenage assistant who came in two afternoons a week to earn extra credit for her journalism class. Caroline used her to proof copy occasionally, but mostly she filed or ran errands for John. And went for coffee for those who wanted something other than the thick black goop John brewed.

"A caramel latte," Caroline said.

"Nonfat milk, medium?"

"You got it. I'm a creature of habit."

"In the old days reporters all lived on straight black coffee," John said.

"Yeah, yeah, we know," one of the grunt reporters said. "And walked a mile in the snow barefoot to get a good story."

That brought a rumble of laughter. Caroline went back to her typing. She was trying to stretch five good sentences from one of Sally's friends from Auburn into half a column. She didn't know about the old days, but being a reporter these days was tough enough.

Ron Baker stopped by her desk, which he made a habit of doing a couple of times a day when she was in the office. She usually didn't mind. He was even newer at the paper than she was and didn't quite fit into the camaraderie routine yet.

Fitting in was always harder for the nonreporters, but Ron was nice. Pushing fifty, a little shy, but a hard worker. His main job was seeing that the newspapers got to the carriers and the dispensers every morning, but he was a kind of jack-of-all-trades and

John took advantage of all his skills. Today he was putting up some new shelves in the supply room.

Ron looked over her shoulder. "You must get tired of writing about that murder every day."

"I wouldn't, if there were something new to say."

"No new leads, huh?"

"If there are, the cops are keeping the news to themselves."

"What do you think of that detective they put in charge of the case? Sam…something or other."

"Turner." What did she think of Sam Turner? Now that was an interesting question. Rude. Irritable. And sexy. "I haven't been around him enough to form an opinion yet."

"Not doing much about finding the killer, is he?"

"Hopefully there's more progress than we know about."

Ron nodded. "Guess I better get back to my shelves."

But after he left, the question of Sam Turner stayed on her mind. Maybe she should do an article on him. He was certainly fascinating in his own way. Kind of a man's man, but there had been that minute in the park when he'd picked up on her fear and had actually seemed protective. And the way he'd looked at her when she'd first opened the door in the satin dress had been a little heated. He'd recovered fast, though.

The bottom line was that he was all business. Which probably wasn't a bad thing when there was a killer on the loose. She just needed to remember that any interest he showed in her was all business, too.

She still had Sam's card in her pocket, but fortunately she hadn't had to call him to report any more contact from the weirdo who might or might not have been the killer.

But since she had his card in her pocket, perhaps she should call him. She was a reporter, after all, and he was the detective in charge. If he had new information, the public had a right to know. And this wasn't because now that she was thinking about him, she really wanted to hear his voice or have him suggest they get together. Sure he was sexy and masculine to the core, but this was business. All business.

She pulled the card from her handbag, checked the number and punched it in.

"Sam Turner."

"Hi, Sam."

"Who is this?"

"Caroline Kimberly, reporter with the *Prentice Times.*"

"What's wrong?"

The concern in his voice surprised her and made her feel a little guilty for calling the number he'd given her to use in case of an emergency. But she'd called, so she had to say something.

"Nothing's wrong. I was just working on an article for tomorrow's paper and I thought you might have a statement to make."

"If you want a statement, call someone in PR."

"I've tried that. There is no one in PR, only whoever happens to be manning the phones." The silence grew awkward. "I'm sorry if I caught you at a bad time."

"You didn't. I mean you did, but I don't know

when a good time would be. The only statement I can make is we haven't made an arrest.''

"Does that mean you have a suspect, or suspects?" She was really pushing it now.

"It means I don't have a statement except that we haven't made an arrest.''

"Okay. I'm sorry I bothered you.''

"Yeah.''

The man's conversation skills were abysmal.

"If you get any more messages," he said, "call me immediately. It's important that you do that. Don't play with this guy, Caroline. He's dangerous. Remember that.''

There was the concern again. Sam Turner was a hard man to figure.

"I promise I'll call. I'm just your basic coward when it comes to dealing with murderers.''

"Good. Cowards have a much better chance of living to old age.''

She thanked him again, said goodbye, and that was the end of that. Feat accomplished. Results nil. Still, Sam stayed on her mind.

"Do you have that copy for me?" John asked, stopping at her desk with cup of goop in hand.

"Give me twenty minutes.''

"Make it ten. You write too much filler, anyway. Cut to the chase. It makes what you have to say more powerful.''

She went back to her typing, but it dawned on her that perhaps Sam should have been a reporter. If fewer words translated to powerful, he'd have won a Pulitzer.

CAROLINE BREATHED a sigh of relief as she pulled the car into her garage and killed the engine. It had been a long day and she was ready to slip out of the black pumps that were starting to squeeze her toes, pour a nice cold glass of chardonnay and watch a rerun of *Will and Grace.*

The garage, a fairly recent addition, sat a few yards behind the two-story house in the spot where a carriage house had been. The walk from the car to her back door was a pain when the weather was cold or rainy, but tonight it was clear and the brisk air felt good.

Only, tonight the area next to the garage was darker than usual. Much darker. For some reason, neither of her outdoor lights were burning, though they were on a timer and should have switched on at dusk. Probably a temporary power outage had them off schedule. Fortunately, she'd left the outdoor light over the back door on so she'd at least be able to see well enough to fit the key into the lock.

Something moved in the bushes behind her. Her heart slammed against her chest, but when she turned, it was only a cat that she'd startled from the bushes. Constant talk of murder had her spooked.

As she neared the house, she noticed a small package propped against the back door. She stopped in her tracks. The package was probably perfectly harmless, but no one had ever left one there before.

What if it had been delivered by the same man who'd left the note on her windshield? He knew what kind of car she drove. Maybe he also knew where she lived. He could be here now, lurking somewhere in the shadows and watching her the way he'd obviously watched her that night in the park. She couldn't see him, but it was almost as if she could feel his presence.

Her heart pounded so loudly that if he was anywhere near, he could surely hear it. Probably even smell her fear. A killer. And her only defense against him and his knife were the keys in her shaking hand.

And there was nowhere to run.

Chapter Four

Caroline made a dash for the door. So far, so good, but her hands were shaking so badly that she had to try twice to get the key into the lock. Finally she was able to turn it. The door swung open and she rushed inside, giving the package a kick so that it slid across the threshold and onto the tiled kitchen floor.

Once inside, she slammed the door shut and fell against it, twisting both the lock and dead bolt into place. The package was still on the floor. A small white bag, folded over at the top, like the kind that came from McClellan's Bakery. It could be anything, maybe something a neighbor had left. She'd probably overreacted, panicked at nothing. There was only one way to find out.

Still she procrastinated. Instead of opening it, she went to the sink and filled a glass with tap water, letting the cool stream splash over her fingers and hands. She drank every drop, then finally stopped and picked up the white bag.

It weighed only a few ounces. Nothing too dangerous could come in a package that small. She unfolded the top and peeked inside. A cookie. A damn heart-shaped cookie. And she'd practically had a coronary over it. She was definitely not cut out for the crime beat.

She almost laughed as she took the cookie out of the bag, but the sound caught in her throat. Beneath the cookie was a note on the same sort of sticky paper as the one that had been on her windshield.

The cookie slipped from her fingers and fell to the cold ceramic tile, crumbling into a thousand pieces. She picked up the note, holding it by the upper right-hand corner with two shaking fingers.

Hello, my beautiful Caroline. I read your stories about me every day and know you are thinking of me the way I am thinking of you.
Happy Valentine's Day.

"Damn him." She hadn't even remembered that it was Valentine's Day and the only reminder she'd gotten was from a lunatic. She pushed the toe of her shoe into the cookie crumbs and ground them as if she were putting out a lit cigarette, the way she'd like to grind his head. How dare he try to suck her into his twisted life?

But she couldn't let him turn her into a shivering mass of nerves. She'd already spent way too much of her life like that, fighting the demons that lived in her nightmares, remnants of a life she didn't even remember.

Still shaken from the panic, but determined, she crossed the room, picked up the wall phone and dialed Sam's number.

SAM READ THE NOTE for the second time. He'd expected it, just hadn't known precisely when it'd come.

"What do you think?" Caroline asked as he placed the note back into the plastic bag for evidence.

"I think he's one sick bastard."

"But do you think it's really from the man who killed Sally Martin, or just some kook seeking attention?"

"There's no way to be sure, but either way, we have to assume he's dangerous."

"Why does that not make me feel better?"

"You're a smart woman."

"So what do I do, Detective?"

He watched her pad over to the sofa in her bare feet, sit down and curl her feet up under her. She was wearing sweats the color of peaches. She looked incredibly vulnerable, and much too soft to be a reporter.

"You could get the hell out of Dodge. Go somewhere this ghoul can't find you and stay there until he's caught."

"I can't do that."

"Sure you can. All you have to do is give up the story."

"I know what you think of reporters, Sam, but we're not all bottom feeders. The press is important. People do have a right and a responsibility to stay informed."

"You have me all wrong. I don't have anything

against reporters unless they interfere with my doing my job.'' But this wasn't about him. It was about her. ''Your leaving town for a little while won't destroy the free press, Caroline. There are plenty of reporters not being stalked by a lunatic who can handle this assignment.''

She stared into space, frustration etched in the lines of her face. ''Running away is not an option. In the first place, I have nowhere to go and no funds to go on. Secondly, I need this job to pay the bills. Besides, if I leave, who's to say this man won't just find someone else to focus his sick attentions on?''

He couldn't argue that. ''So what's your solution, Caroline? Just go about your business and wait for the next gift, or note, or whatever else he conjures up in his depraved mind?''

''No.'' She met his gaze head-on. ''He obviously reads the newspaper. Maybe I should write an article encouraging him to communicate with me more directly. If I could talk to him, we could set a trap for him.''

Or she could just go out and commit suicide, Sam thought. It would amount to the same thing. ''You'd be playing the killer's game. You think you'll get inside his head, but he'll get inside yours.''

''I'm not a fool, Sam. I won't be manipulated.''

''You already have been.'' His phone rang. He excused himself and went to the kitchen to take the call.

''What's up?'' he asked when one of the cops from the precinct identified himself.

''Just heard from the local TV station. They got another call.''

He muttered a couple of well-chosen curses. "A body?"

"Caller didn't say. Just gave specifics as to where they should go."

"Let's have it."

"Cedar Park. It's on Jackson Avenue, in the Hunter's Grove area. That's where those historic homes are located."

Cedar Park. Three blocks from where he was sitting right now. "I'll be there in five minutes. Call Matt. I want him there, too. And get me a crew to work crime-scene detail."

When he broke the connection, Caroline was standing right behind him.

"He struck again, didn't he."

"They're not sure. I have to go."

"Where?"

He ignored the question. "Stay here and keep your doors locked." He knew that telling her to stay would do about as much good as telling that to the stray dog who'd parked himself on his doorstep.

When he left, she followed him out the door.

"I GOT A COUPLE of great closeups before Officer Friendly herded us back," Steve said. "John's gonna love us." Steve moved his camera from his right shoulder to his left.

Caroline marveled at her photog's enthusiasm for gore. "Nice you could make it this time."

Steve was like a grinning porcupine, with his short piky hair. "Hey, I'd have made it last time if you'd told me what was waiting for me. Doreen always gave me a heads-up on stuff like this.''

"I didn't know what it was the last time, but your job is to come when I call.''

"Okay. Just made that one little slip. Don't have to hit me over the head with it. I'm your guy. Besides, John called before you did tonight. Told me my ass better be here, not that he'll run any of the really good stuff.''

"John must have gotten the word about a second after the TV station did,'' Caroline said.

"Be nice to hear about something *before* the TV folk do every once in a while. But who can compete with TV?'' Steve said. "Hey, let's grab a six-pack and get down to the newspaper office with our goodies.''

"You go ahead.''

"All right. Catch you later,'' he said, and loped away, his long, skinny legs at odds with his fat gut. Steve was only four years younger than she was, but life for him was still a six-pack and a party.

She pulled her jacket tighter as she watched him go, then turned back to the activity in the park. There were only a few guys left. Sam, of course, and a few other cops, some uniformed, some not. Channel Six had left almost immediately, no doubt in time to make the ten-o'clock broadcast with late-breaking news. As usual, the *Prentice Times* would be several hours later with their late-breaking coverage, so she'd be expected to supply a lot more detail.

The second murder was no less gruesome than the first. Outwardly, Caroline had handled it better; though her stomach had heaved, she'd managed not to throw up. Inwardly, she was a wreck. The man who'd committed such a vile act was probably out there right now, watching her.

She leaned against the park fence, a short distance from where Sam was doing his investigation.

The no-nonsense detective hadn't spoken a word to her at the scene, yet he'd acknowledged her presence with his eyes. He'd looked at her again and again, as if making sure she was still there and hadn't gone off with the killer.

Strange. The killer's intention was apparently to draw her into this with him, but instead, she felt she was being drawn into Sam's world, almost as if they were unwilling partners. Same goal, but with conflicting ideas about how to achieve it.

Moments later she felt a hand on her shoulder. "You okay?"

"No."

"Want to get something to eat and talk about it?"

"I want to talk. I'm not sure I can eat."

"I'm famished. The Grille is about the only place open after nine on a weeknight other than the fast-food chains. You can ride with me if you like."

"Come to my house," she surprised herself by saying. "I'll make omelettes. They'll be easier on the digestive tract."

"You sure?"

"Why not?"

"No reason I can think of. Give me a few minutes to finish up here."

"Take your time," she said. "I'll go ahead."

"I'd rather you wait for me."

"Because you think the killer might follow me home?"

He exhaled sharply, as if she was pulling confessions from him. "Just wait for me. I'll follow you back to the house."

She nodded, grateful for the concern and even more for the protection. But it would be only for an hour or so. After that, it'd be open season on her again.

She pulled out her notebook and a pen as Sam walked away and moved within the glow of a streetlight. She'd write her article on her laptop after they finished the omelettes. John could hold off printing the front page for an hour since he knew the copy was coming. She needed to jot down a few notes, but it was the questions that haunted her mind that actually found their way to the pen.

Does the heart of a madman beat faster while he's taking someone's life? Does he get off on the blood? Or is it the terror in the victim's eyes that gives him the sadistic pleasure? And what is it this madman wants from me?

Her fingers began to shake and she dropped the pen. A man who'd been standing nearby picked it up and handed it to her. "Not much reason to hang around now," he said.

Her heart stopped beating for a second, then jumped to her throat. The man just stood there, non-threatening, smiling. She was definitely getting paranoid. This place was crawling with cops. No killer with a shred of sense would show his face here. "Are you with the police department?"

"Yeah. Matt Hastings, homicide detective. And you've got to be a reporter."

"Yes. Caroline Kimberly with the *Prentice Times*. How did you know?"

"Cops can always spot a reporter. Your eyes have that beady vulture glow."

"You're kidding, aren't you?"

"Yeah," he said, his tone growing more friendly. "Sam pointed you out to me. You're the one who got the note."

"Sam told you about that?"

"We're partners on this case." He looked back to where a couple of uniformed cops were stringing the crime-scene tape. "It's pretty much all done around here for the night. You could clear out now and not miss a thing. I can give you a ride home."

"No, thanks. I have my car."

"You must be new at this," he said, lingering. "I don't remember seeing you at any of these soirees before the Sally Martin murder."

"I've been at the newspaper for six months, but I just started getting the crime assignments."

"Lucky you, huh?"

"What do you mean?"

"Two murders in less than a week. Looks like you may just have yourself a serial killer."

"I could have done without it," she said.

"All the same, a story like this can make a new reporter. Get you noticed by one of the big dailies, maybe even one of the TV channels."

"I'm not even sure I'm up to *this* job."

"Hey, Matt," one of other officers hollered from several yards away. "Sam's looking for you."

"Duty calls," Matt said. "Nice to have you around. You do a lot to brighten up a crime scene."

Her fingers fumbled with the notebook as she found her place again. But this time it was Matt's words she jotted onto the page. *You've got yourself a serial killer.*

How did she get so lucky?

SAM SAT at the kitchen table, drinking a Scotch while Caroline broke eggs into a mixing bowl. He was dead tired, but not sleepy. He could never sleep after a murder. The details always ran in his mind like a movie trailer. Tonight was no exception. Only, tonight Caroline was the central figure in half the scenes.

The timing of the cookie delivery and tonight's murder strengthened his belief that the man stalking Caroline was the actual killer. It was the cause and effect he wasn't clear on. Had the crackpot just noticed her in that red dress at the scene of the first murder and been attracted to her? Had he killed tonight just to see her again?

But then, he didn't have to kill to see her. He knew where she worked, what car she drove and where she lived. Plain and simple, he was stalking her. But maybe stalking was the prelude to his murders. He could be stalking several women, getting his rocks off watching them and frightening them. Then at some point that only he knew was coming, he killed them.

The chief would want a profiler in. Sam didn't have anything against profilers, but he didn't like them on his cases. They tended to narrow the field of suspects far too much.

Inexperienced cops tended to overlook suspects who strayed too far outside the artificial boundaries the profilers set up for them. And if the profiler was wrong, citizens were wary of the wrong guys and frequently left themselves exposed to the real danger. It had happened to him once in the early days.

Caroline opened the refrigerator door, leaned over and rummaged through one of the compartments. The soft fabric of her sweatpants draped across her buttocks, outlining them so that the lines of her panties showed. Bikini, cut high—and low. His body reacted swiftly, a twinge he wouldn't have thought it capable of after the past two hours.

"I can make a Spanish omelet if you like," she said. "Or just ham and mushrooms. Your call."

"Let's go with the Spanish. No mushrooms. No spinach or any of that other rabbit food, either."

"Not a health-food nut I take it."

"No. Beer nuts is as healthy as I get. Need some help?"

"You could build a fire in the fireplace in the drawing room. And set up the card table so we can eat in there."

"The drawing room?"

"Second door off the front hall," she said. "One of the few rooms with furniture. Most people would call it a living room, I guess, or a family room. The original house plans refer to it as a drawing room, and I like the sound of that."

"Then we shall dine in the drawing room," he

said, faking a sophisticated drawl. It sounded more like a poor comic routine.

"There are logs on the grate and kindling in a basket on the hearth."

"No gas starter?"

"Afraid not. Doesn't fit with the idea of historic preservation." She nudged the refrigerator door closed with her hip, her hands overflowing with sausage, cheese, bell peppers and onions. He rushed over to help her, putting his hands under hers to catch the onion just before it rolled from her grasp. They both backed away at the same time, as if the mere meeting of their hands had caused an electrical shock. He laid the onion on the table.

"I'll get the fire started."

"Okay. And the card table's in the hall closet. Don't bother with the chairs. We can use the ones in the drawing room."

He escaped the kitchen and the crackle of whatever had happened between them. When he did, his pulse returned to normal. Only, sensual sparks were like a called third strike in the bottom of the ninth of a losing game. They hung around to haunt you.

He found the drawing room. He'd expected a large open space. The room was actually cozy with lots of old photographs on the walls, comfortable chairs under the tall windows and an antique organ in one corner. He stooped in front of the hearth, rearranged the logs to his liking, then struck a match to the kindling.

The fire caught quickly, shooting flames to lick at the logs. A crackling fire in the drawing room. A beautiful woman cooking in the kitchen.

And a killer walking the streets of Prentice, Georgia.

He shook himself. He had to keep his mind on what really mattered here, and that wasn't his libido. He had a murderer to catch. And a spunky reporter to keep safe.

CAROLINE SAT ACROSS from Sam, nibbling a slice of toast she'd made from a loaf of crusty bread she'd picked up yesterday at McClellan's Bakery.

She and Sam had talked little during the meal. She imagined he was as hesitant as she was to spoil the food with talk of bodies and killers. But they were basically through eating now, and the silence had grown awkward.

"Do you live here alone?" he asked, finishing his second Scotch of the evening.

"Except for the ghosts, and they don't help any with the housework or expenses."

"Ghosts? Don't tell me you believe in that unearthly hype?"

"Are you so sure they don't exist?"

"I don't really care if they do or not. As long as they don't commit crimes on my turf."

"I'm not sure they exist, either," she admitted, sipping a glass of wine that she hoped would help her sleep tonight. "But if they do, I think this would be the ideal place for them."

"So why did you buy the house?"

"I didn't. I leased it from Barkley Billingham. The Billingham family were the original owners, and that's one of the reasons I like the house. It cradles a family's past."

"But you're not a Billingham. So it's not your history."

"They've adopted me, or I've adopted them. I'm not sure which. Not legally, of course, but since I've moved in, I feel connected to them, especially to Frederick. He was the builder of this grand old house."

Sam frowned. "Do you feel that same kind of connection to the killer?"

"What kind of question is that?"

"A fair one, under the circumstances."

"If you're asking do I somehow feel responsible for his killing that girl tonight, the answer is no. But I do keep wondering why he's fixated on me. I think he may be calling out to me for help."

"He doesn't need your help. He needs to be arrested, and you need to take a break from the newspaper until he's behind bars."

"That's not the way I see it."

"Then you better get some glasses to help your vision. You can have all the connections you want with the Billingham ghosts, Caroline. Sleep with them. Eat with them. Have tea with them in your drawing room. That's your decision. But connecting with the man who carved up his second victim tonight comes under the heading of my business. And I'm not going to just stand by and watch you get sucked in by this man."

"You surely don't think I'm developing some kind of improper fascination with the monster, do you?"

"Yeah, I do."

She took a deep breath and let it out slowly, expelling the steam that was building inside her. "I'm not stealing your case from you, Sam, if that's what you're worried about. I won't print anything he tells me without talking to you first."

He threw up his hands. "See? You're already thinking about talking to the man. You'll probably invite him in for tea if he shows up at your door tonight. Make him an omelette. Hell, maybe he can just spend the night."

The memory of finding the package at her door flashed in her mind. The terror returned with the image, and a cold shiver trailed her spine and brought a spattering of gooseflesh to her arms.

"I'm sorry, Caroline."

The apology was unexpected, though his voice was still gruff with the anger that had driven him moments ago. Or was it something else that strained his voice? She started to pick up her napkin, then realized her hands were shaking.

"I don't want to fight, Sam. I can't. Not tonight. I just can't take any more tonight."

A second later he was beside her, pulling her up into his arms. Her emotions were all mixed up. Fear. Anger. Need. She started to push him away, but his lips were mere inches away, his breath hot on her flesh.

She knotted her fingers in the front of his shirt, pulling instead of pushing, caught up in a hunger that was so new and unexpected she didn't begin to understand it.

And then Sam's lips touched hers and the hunger exploded into flames.

Chapter Five

Sam's body pressed against Caroline's as his mouth claimed hers. She was consumed by the kiss and her need to be feel something warm and passionate that didn't begin and end with terror. The kiss was too sudden, too unexpected, yet she gave in to it so fully that she was trembling when Sam pulled away.

"I didn't mean to do that."

She stepped back and caught her breath, smoothing the front of her shirt with the flat of her hands. "Hey, no big deal," she lied, her heart still pounding and her body weak from the onslaught of unexpected emotions. "You don't have to apologize."

"I'm not sorry I kissed you. I just didn't plan for it to happen—not like that."

She had no idea what he meant. Was it the timing or the intensity he hadn't expected, or was it her response? It didn't matter. The mood was broken and she felt awkward talking about it after the fact. Kisses like that weren't supposed to be analyzed like evidence at a crime scene.

"I think you should go now," she said. "I have to write the copy for tomorrow's headline story."

"Yeah. Gotta keep the public informed."

She leaned over and blew out the candle in the center of the table, then started clearing away the plates.

"I'll help with the dishes," Sam offered.

"No. I'll just rinse them tonight." She didn't want his help, didn't want to risk his getting too close again. Her emotions were raw, and if they kissed again, things might get out of hand.

Sam picked up the empty glasses and followed her to the kitchen. "What kind of locks do you have on your doors and windows?"

His voice was all business. From passion to cop in far less time than it was taking her heart to still. "The outside doors have dead bolts. The windows have standard locks. I had them all checked when I moved in."

"Are they all locked now?"

"I keep them locked, except when I open them to let in fresh air."

"Good."

His concern sparked a nebulous dread that seemed to choke the oxygen from the room. "You think the killer may be planning for me to be one of his victims, don't you?"

He leaned against the counter and faced her. "I can't read this guy, Caroline. All I know is what I've seen of his handiwork, and that's enough reason for me not to take chances with your life."

"But you talk as if the note and cookie are part of some kind of weird foreplay. That's not how he works, Sam. The other women had no history with him."

"That we know of. Dead women don't talk."

Crapola! She hadn't thought of that. The forks slipped from her hands, clattering into the sink.

"There will be a surveillance cop watching your house tonight and every night until this guy is arrested. He won't stay parked in the same spot all the time, but he'll be out there somewhere. If there's any problem at all, even if you hear a noise that's unfamiliar, call 911. The patrolman can get to you almost instantly."

"How do you know?"

"Because I've already talked to the chief and he's okayed it. It will keep you safe and help us find the killer if he's snooping around. Now I need to go and let you get your story written."

And that was Sam. Hard to figure. Tough, but protective. Hot one minute, cold the next. Sensual, then detached, as if he peeked out from behind some invisible barrier only to crawl back behind when she got too close.

"You better go," she said, "before the patrolman on watch sees your car and wonders what you're up to."

He smiled. "He's probably already wondering that."

She walked him to the door.

"There he is," Sam said.

She scanned the street. Sure enough, a squad car was parked three doors down, beneath a magnolia tree. She breathed a grateful sigh. "Thanks, Detective."

"You're welcome, Reporter."

For a split second she thought he might kiss her

again, but he turned and walked away, his feet clapping on the wooden steps. Heavy. Solid. Not at all like her ghosts, but she liked the sound.

SAM WAS WIDE AWAKE as he left Caroline's and climbed behind the wheel of his unmarked car. He stopped for a minute and chatted with the surveillance cop, then drove back to Cedar Park. He wanted to see it deserted, the way it had probably been when the killer struck.

He parked by the gate, but didn't get out of the car. The park wasn't lighted, but the night was clear and moonlight dappled the shadowed area with splotches of illumination.

Hopefully by tomorrow morning the victim would be positively identified. Then he'd have the miserable task of going to the family. He could send someone else, but those first moments of grief were frequently the telling ones, when everyone's guard was down.

There were little things he might pick up about the latest victim's lifestyle, unexpected clues as to how she became the target of the killer. But he wouldn't be looking for signs of guilt among the family members this time. While he couldn't rule out a copycat murder, it was highly likely that the crime had been committed by the same man who'd killed Sally Martin. Cruel murder by a man with no conscience.

The way it had been with Peg.

His heart constricted as if someone were squeezing the valves and shutting it down. Time was supposed to heal all wounds, so said the all-knowing shrink the San Antonio police chief had made him see before he'd finally left there and moved back to Georgia. But seven years hadn't done a lot toward dulling the memory or the pain.

It might have been different if he'd gotten some kind of closure. But he hadn't. The guy who'd killed Peg had never been caught, even though Sam had been so obsessed with finding him that he'd lost his job. Even that hadn't stopped him. Finally booze had.

Realizing he was turning into a bitter drunk, just like the stepfather he'd hated so much, he'd cleaned up his act and gotten a job with the Prentice Police Department, thanks to a recommendation from his old supervisor. Tony Sistrunk had probably saved his life.

Sam had come a long way since then. But these two murders brought it all back home. Two women had died needlessly, throats slashed and chests painted by some crazy punk with a knife.

And it wasn't enough that he killed without cause. No, he had to be mesmerized by Caroline Kimberly, a woman who'd already managed to crawl under Sam's skin the way no woman had done in seven long years.

Caroline had probably hit close to the truth with her analogy. Tonight she'd probably been the foreplay. The latest victim had been the orgasm. But how long would that be enough?

Sam started the engine and drove away with Peg and the pain of losing her in his heart, a killer on his mind. And the taste of a feisty, sexy reporter still clinging to his lips.

THE GHOSTS WERE out in force tonight, creaking floorboards and moaning with the wind as it rounded the corner outside Caroline's bedroom. The noises of the old house were familiar. She knew it was crazy, but even if the spirits were only imagined, she liked thinking they were there. A link to the past. A sense of continuity that eased the loneliness that came from a life of belonging nowhere and to no one.

She'd been placed in the Grace Girls' Home when she was seven. She'd been treated well there, but being treated well wasn't the same as being part of a family. She didn't remember anything before being at Grace. But by the time she moved there, the nightmare that still haunted her was already in place.

A church. Dark, steep stairs that led to a bottomless pit. The fear that she was going into that hell and would never come out. And the sound of a crying baby. Probably memories she'd locked away, a school counselor had once told her. If so, she hoped they stayed locked away forever.

And now she'd have the sights of murdered women and a heart-shaped cookie in a white paper bag to add to the cache of things better forgotten. She shivered just thinking about opening the bag and seeing the note. It had been only a few hours since she'd found it by her back door, yet so much had happened since then.

The murder.

And the surprise of the evening—Sam's kiss.

Not that the kiss had been bad. To the contrary, she'd liked it a lot. Even when he was being a pain, Sam had a kind of brooding sex appeal that was impossible to deny.

She wondered what might have happened if he hadn't pulled away when he had. Would she have stopped him before they went too far, or would he be in bed beside her now? She honestly didn't know.

Caroline closed her eyes and began counting backward from a hundred, the way she did when she had trouble falling asleep. By the time she reached seventy-seven, her thoughts were drifting aimlessly, in and out of her consciousness, and she fell into a restless sleep.

The images crept in. Sam's lips on hers, his hands in her hair, her heart beating fast. Too fast. He faded away and there was the cookie staring at her, sitting next to a bloody body.

She tossed and turned, the dream moving through space and time until she was a little girl, holding hands and giggling with her friends. But she was cold. And it was dark.

And then the baby started to cry.

Caroline jerked awake, an old familiar fear choking her. She threw her legs over the side of the bed, stuffed her feet into her fuzzy slippers and started to the kitchen for a glass of water.

Her bedroom was downstairs, at the end of the wide hallway. She hurried past the door to the basement, but still felt the cold draft that was always there. It was the only part of the old house she didn't like. She'd started for water, but she paused at the foot of the winding staircase. The entire house held the essence of the Billinghams, but their spirits always seemed more pronounced upstairs.

Caroline climbed the steps slowly, turned on the overhead chandelier and breathed a little easier as the antique brass fixture sprayed the wide, second-floor hallway with a glow filtered through faceted crystal.

The grandfather clock downstairs struck three. Too early to start the day, but Caroline didn't want to go back to the bedroom, so she curled up on the old sofa and pulled the patterned quilt over her legs. This time she slept till morning.

CAROLINE WAS at her desk in the *Times* office two days later, putting the finishing touches on a story about the reflections of the residents near Cedar Park concerning the brutal crime that had been committed in their historic and usually quiet neighborhood—and against one of their own. The victim had been identified as Ruby Givens, a twenty-six-year-old unmarried nurse who'd gone for a late evening jog.

Caroline had spent the morning interviewing the people who lived on the street bordering the park, and in every case she could see fear in their eyes. Most didn't want to be mentioned in the article by name. Anonymity seemed safest to those too close to the crime.

The people in the area knew a lot more about the viciousness of the crime than they would have if the news media had not been first on the scene. The police hadn't gotten a chance to run the information through their filter system before it was released.

Indications were that the killer was the man who'd called both the TV station and the newspaper offices. Apparently he craved the spotlight. As yet that was all anyone seemed to know about him, unless the police had leads they weren't revealing.

But Sam's words played in her mind the way they had all day today. *Dead women don't talk.* Could that have anything to do with why they were dead? Had the killer stalked them, tried to get them to go out with him and been rejected? But if that had been the case with Sally Martin, why hadn't her family mentioned it?

Duh. Who told their parents about guys hitting on them? But Sally would have told someone. Women always talked. So why hadn't her friends told the police?

Fear. The same fear that had been so prominent in the people Caroline had interviewed this morning. The kind of fear that had turned her into a shuddering mass at the sight of a package by her door.

Maybe she should go back to the Catfish Shack and see if she could catch Trudy Mitchell. Trudy and Sally were about the same age. Both were employees at the restaurant, and come to think of it, Trudy had seemed nervous when Caroline had interviewed her right after Sally's murder. But then, so had everyone else.

The phone on her desk buzzed. Light three was blinking. She picked up the receiver. "Caroline Kimberly, news desk."

"So what's the news these days?"

"Hi, Becky. I was just thinking about calling you."

"Have you had lunch yet?"

"I grabbed a burger on my way back to the office."

"Ugh. Greasy fast food when you could have stopped by Bon Appetit. You could come out now for coffee and dessert."

"Sounds good, but I have a story to finish for tomorrow's edition."

"Then how about tennis tomorrow?"

She chuckled at Becky and her boundless energy, but Caroline could use the exercise. "Tennis sounds wonderful."

"Super. Is ten okay? We can meet at the club."

"I'll see you there."

Becky had the life. She owned Bon Appetit, a small coffeehouse and gourmet deli that was always busy—not that Becky needed the money. But she could go in and work when she wanted or hang out at the Prentice Country Club and play tennis whenever the mood hit her.

She had a great family, too. No brothers or sisters, but Dr. and Mrs. Simpson were as sweet as they could be, and they doted on their vivacious daughter. The only thing Becky didn't have in her life was a steady boyfriend. But there was plenty of time, even though Becky wanted a houseful of kids. She was only twenty-six.

The same age as Ruby Givens. So back to the article and the gore.

THE CATFISH SHACK was located about ten miles southwest of town, off Highway 5 and overlooking the Chattahoochee River. It was too late for the lunch crowd and too early for the dinner crowd when Caroline arrived. A perfect time for talking to the blond bartender.

Caroline scanned the restaurant. There was a family with three small children sitting at a back table, an elderly couple sitting next to the window and a couple of guys in hunting attire sitting smack in the middle of the room. That was, no doubt, their mud-caked vehicle she'd parked next to in the parking lot.

"You can sit anywhere," a middle-aged waitress said, scooting by her with a platter of golden-fried catfish. Caroline opted for the bar and had her choice of stools. Prentice was not a drinking town, especially before quitting time on a Friday afternoon. She waited for several minutes before Trudy came out of the kitchen and spotted her.

Trudy frowned as she walked over. "Are you here to drink or to ask questions?"

"I'll have a cup of coffee."

Trudy was attractive even in a uniform that did nothing for her slim figure. She didn't smile or make eye contact when she set the coffee in front of Caroline.

"Cream?"

"No. I'll take it black."

Trudy picked up a damp rag and started wiping the counter, ignoring Caroline, but staying within speaking distance.

Caroline was almost certain she wasn't going to get any more information from Trudy than what she'd gotten the last time, but she might as well give it a shot.

"Had you known Sally long?"

Trudy wiped all the harder on a surface that was already glossy. "I didn't know her until she came to work here."

"How long ago was that?"

"About six months ago." She dropped the cloth and held on to the edge of the bar. "Guess that was her big mistake."

An odd response. Unless, of course, Sally's working here had something to do with her death. Maybe she'd met the killer here. But then, if Trudy thought that, she must have an idea who the perp was. "Did Sally date much?"

"You asked me that the last time. I told you then I don't know anything about who she dated or where she went when she left here. We were friendly at work, but we didn't hang out together."

Caroline nodded. Wrong approach. She needed to be less direct. Had to consider the fear factor. "The catfish smell good. I don't how you manage your weight so well working here."

"I don't eat the catfish. I look at it and smell it all day. That's enough."

"But I bet the tips are good."

"Good enough. Not as good as they were when I worked some of the nightspots in Atlanta."

"But at least it's a family place so you don't have guys hitting on you all the time like you would in a big city."

"You'd think."

"Doesn't work that way, huh?"

"Not always."

Trudy looked away, but she was biting her lip, and Caroline was almost certain she'd hit a nerve. "Bet Sally had a few admirers, pretty as she was."

"She had them." Trudy walked over and refilled Caroline's coffee cup. "Are you thinking that one of the guys who came in here might have killed her?"

"I don't know enough to even venture a guess. What do you think?"

Trudy didn't say a word, but Caroline read the

answer in her eyes and the way her hand shook when she put the coffeepot back in place.

Now was the time to push. "Your co-worker is dead, Trudy, and so is another young woman. If you know anything that might lead to finding the guy responsible, you owe it to both of them to say so."

Trudy picked up the cloth again, but this time she only wrung it in her hands. "I don't know anything."

"I know it's scary, but you can level with me. I'm not a cop."

"Same difference. If I tell you something, it goes right in the newspaper for everyone in town to read."

"It doesn't have to."

"What do you mean?"

"Just what I said. I won't print it if you don't want me to."

"But you'd tell that detective who keeps coming around."

"Detective Turner?"

"Him and the young detective who works with him."

"Matt?"

"Yeah. He comes here almost every day. All the waitresses like him. But I've told him time and again I don't know anything."

"If you tell me, I can give them the information without letting everyone know you're the one who told me."

"Wouldn't you have to if they asked?"

"A reporter never has to reveal her sources." That wasn't entirely true, but in this case it wouldn't matter. "I'd only give the information to Detective

Turner, and he isn't going to leak the information, Sally. He's not going to endanger you.''

"How do I know I can trust you?"

"Because I'm a woman, too. I feel the same fear you do and I won't put you at risk." Caroline's pulse quickened. "Was someone stalking Sally?"

"No. Nothing like that." Trudy leaned in close and lowered her voice to a whisper. "But there was this one guy who came in all the time. He never ordered food, just hung around the bar and talked to Sally when she'd go back and forth to the kitchen. He watched her, too. All the time."

"What was his name?"

"I don't know."

Caroline was sure she was lying again. "A name would really help."

"I don't know his name."

"Was he Sally's boyfriend?"

"No. She was still hung up on some guy at Auburn. They'd had a thing while she was in school there, but he'd broken up with her. That's when she flunked out and came home."

Caroline wondered if Sam knew about the guy at Auburn. She was almost certain he didn't know about the guy who hung out at the Catfish Shack. "Do you think Sally ever saw this guy away from the restaurant?"

"I don't think so, but I'm not sure."

"How old is this guy?"

"Late twenties, maybe."

"Has he been in here since Sally was killed?"

Trudy backed away and went back to scrubbing the bar. "I don't know. I don't know anything else."

Caroline reached across the bar and laid her hand on Trudy's. It was cold as ice. "Tell me what the guy looks like, Trudy. I promise he won't find out that you told me."

"He's nice-looking. Blond hair. Wears it short."

"How tall?"

"I'm not good at heights."

"Taller than you?"

"Oh, yeah. Average, I'd say, for a guy."

"Is he slim?"

"No. Average. He's just pretty much average, except on the cute side if you consider most of the guys around Prentice." She leaned her elbows on the bar.

"How did he dress?"

"Slacks and a sport shirt usually. Sometimes jeans."

Caroline scribbled down some notes, then stuck the pad and pen back into the side pocket of her handbag. The description would fit about half the population of Georgia.

"There is one other thing," Trudy said. "I don't think he's from Prentice."

"Why do you say that?"

"Well, I never saw him around town, just in here."

Very interesting. "Thanks, Trudy."

"Remember your promise. I didn't say nothin'."

"You have my word."

Caroline paid for the coffee, left a more-than-generous tip and hurried out to her car. The second she was inside, she took out her cell phone and punched in Sam's number. Busy. She put the phone away and reversed out of the parking spot.

The road back to the highway was short but fairly isolated. Not many houses, and the few that were there sat back near the river and were barely visible through the thick growth of trees.

When her phone rang, Caroline grabbed it, hoping it was Sam, that he'd picked up her number from a calls-missed message. She couldn't keep the excitement from her voice when she answered.

The caller wasn't Sam.

"Hello, Caroline. Did you enjoy your cookie?"

Chapter Six

Caroline switched the phone to "speaker" to free her hands for maneuvering the winding road. The caller's voice was low and guttural, as if he was talking through a device to alter his voice. Her flesh grew clammy, and when she tried to respond to his question, her throat closed on the words.

"I asked if you enjoyed your cookie. It's not polite to ignore a friendly question."

"Y-yes." She had to get control. If he knew how badly he was getting to her, it would give him even more power. "Why did you buy me a cookie?"

"It was Valentine's Day, and I wanted you to know I was thinking of you. Have you been thinking of me, Caroline?"

"Who are you? How did you get my address and my cell-phone number?"

"Oh, sweet, innocent Caroline. You have so much to learn. A smart man can find out anything about anyone. And I am very, very smart."

"Why did you call me?"

"To hear your voice."

"Why? What do you want from me?"

"I must go now, Caroline."

"No. Please don't break the connection. We need to talk. Let me help you."

But the connection went dead, even as the voice still filled her mind like some invisible, poisonous smoke. She turned up the heat in the car, but she doubted the higher temperature would reach the chill that had embedded her heart.

Her phone rang again. Dread consumed her so that she could barely think. She didn't want to talk to him again, yet she might be the only one who could reach him, the only one who could stop him from killing again. She forced herself to pick up the phone, but this time it was Sam's cell number that came up on the viewer handset.

"Thank goodness it's you," she said, skipping the perfunctory hello.

"Are you all right?"

"Yes—and no. I need to talk to you, Sam."

"I'm listening."

"I'd rather not do it over the phone."

"Where are you?"

"Close to the junction of Finnegan Road and Highway 5."

"Near the Catfish Shack."

It was a statement, not a question, and she heard the vexation in his voice. "Don't lecture me, Sam. I'm in no mood for it. Your job is to interrogate. Mine is to interview, and if that puts us on the same turf, so be it. Now, do you have time to see me? It's important."

"Do you know how to get to the police firing range?"

"I've seen the sign. I've never been there."

"It's easy to find. Just stay on Highway 5 back toward town and turn on the road by the sign. It's a rectangular metal building about a mile off the highway. You can't miss it."

"Are you there now?"

"Yeah. When you get here, just ask the guy on duty at the front desk to get me."

"I should be there in ten minutes."

"Are you sure you're all right?"

"I'm in a car going sixty miles an hour and not a killer in sight." Not that it meant he wasn't somewhere nearby. But she doubted seriously he'd follow her to a place where cops had their guns out and were practicing their shooting skills.

So now she had only Sam to deal with—a formidable task indeed.

SAM PULLED the target in close to check his accuracy. Most of his shots had hit the paper cutout in the dead center of the brain, as they should have at the distance he was practicing. He always did some distance firing, as well, but every time he'd ever faced an armed assailant, it had been at almost point-blank range.

He wasn't really here to practice. It was just that sometimes the routine of loading and shooting had a calming effect on him that let him think more clearly, especially when he was as tired as he was today.

He hadn't slept more than a couple of hours a night since the second murder. He'd go to bed only to have the few facts they knew about the killings march though his mind like a parade of the macabre.

Two murders in two different parks. One of the Atlanta TV reporters had already dubbed the murderer the Prentice Park Killer, and the name appeared to have stuck.

The victims seemingly had nothing in common except that they were young women who had been found dead in parks. One had apparently been abducted from the parking lot of her apartment building. One had been attacked while she was jogging on a marked trail that cut through an isolated area of Cedar Park.

They'd both had their throats slit, then been stripped naked and had bloody X's painted across their chests. No sign of sexual molestation. No witnesses. No obvious motives. No leads. And no matter how many people he talked to or how many times he went over all this in his mind, he never got any closer to identifying a killer.

It had been the same today while he'd interviewed Ruby Givens's family. There had to be something he was overlooking, some link that would make all this connect. It appeared the crimes had been committed by the same person, but it was impossible to be certain. Since everything about the first murder had been described in detail on TV and in the paper, the second could easily have been a copycat.

Sam toyed with the facts, moving them around like marbles as he reloaded his gun, a semiautomatic Smith and Wesson. His wasn't standard issue, but he'd requested and gotten permission to use it. It was the same type of gun he'd carried when he'd first signed on as a cop back in San Antonio. He liked the feel of it and knowing exactly how it handled.

"Hey, Sam. Some woman's here to see you. Cute little brunette."

"Get her a pair of earplugs and send her back here."

"Okay, but don't shoot her. She's too good-looking to lose. How about I bring her back and you introduce us?"

"You're looking for me to help you score with a cute chick who asked for me?"

The cop nodded. Sam grinned. "You're out of luck." He tore down the old target, attached a new one and moved it back to the fifteen-foot mark. When he turned around again, Caroline was standing a couple of feet behind him.

No wonder she'd gotten the young cop's attention. She was wearing a yellow sweater that draped over her breasts, outlining her nipples. Not clingy, but seductive all the same. Her straight black skirt stopped just above her knees, and a pair of stylish black boots did great things for her legs.

"You look nice," he said, realizing he was staring.

"Thanks."

"But you didn't just drop by to let me gawk."

"Not really." She looked around, watched the cop next to him fire a couple of rounds, then grimaced. "Can we go somewhere quieter?"

"In a minute." He motioned her closer. He was eager to hear what she had to say, but he also needed to know if she could handle a weapon, and there might not be a better time than now to find out. "Have you ever fired a gun before?"

"No."

"Come here and give it a try."

She shook her head. "I don't like guns."

"You don't have to like them, but under the circumstances, it would be a good idea if you knew how to use one."

"I don't think I could bring myself to shoot someone."

"Most people think that. They don't find out differently until that split second when they have to choose between shooting or getting shot." He took her hand and tugged her closer. "First you need to hold the pistol in your hand for a few minutes. Get used to the feel of it. And always remember that you never point a weapon at anything or anyone you don't intend to shoot."

He placed the gun in her hand and moved her fingers into position. "You can steady the shooting hand with your free hand." He was standing behind her, and when he leaned in to help her with her grip, his chin brushed her hair and he caught the scent of her perfume. Something light and flowery—and intoxicating.

His body reacted swiftly, traitorously growing hard. He kept his hand on hers, but he pulled back, fighting the desire that just wouldn't let up. Whatever it was that fired his libido, Caroline had it in spades.

"Do I pull the trigger now?" she asked.

Her voice trembled a little. Sam had no clue if the tremble was because of the gun or an awareness of what she was doing to him. He wasn't about to ask.

"Use the front and rear sights to help you line up the target. Aim at the head."

She followed his instructions, squinting as she did so. "Now?"

"Whenever you're ready."

She closed her eyes, made a face and pulled the trigger. The bullet missed the target altogether.

She opened her eyes and swung around, pointing the gun directly at him. He took her arm and pushed it away. "You want to watch that, unless you're planning to shoot me."

"I knew I'd be no good at this."

"It takes time."

"I don't even see my bullet hole."

"Hard to aim with your eyes closed."

"Okay, let me try it again. I'll keep them open this time."

"Take it slow and make the shot count."

"Do you suppose the deranged killer who's running around town will stand still for five minutes while I aim?"

"I'm not even considering the possibility that you'll have to find out."

She looked at him. "You don't lie well, Sam."

"It's my only weakness."

She aimed the gun and pulled the trigger, this time keeping her eyes open and her hands reasonably steady. The bullet hit the right forearm of the paper man.

"You're getting closer."

She shot twice more, each one getting a little nearer the prime target spot. She was improving, but she'd need a lot more than a day's practice before he'd want to turn her loose with a weapon. As unsure as she was now, an attacker would take it away from her before she knew what was happening.

"Let's call it a day," he said. "Go have that conversation you came for."

"Good." She looked around. "How far do we have to go?"

"Outside."

He holstered his gun, then removed the target and disposed of it in the open trash barrel. Once out the front door, he led her away from the building and down a path that meandered to a stocked pond, where some of the cops went fishing on their day off.

"It's nice here," she said, "once you get away from the gunfire."

"The land and the building were donated by the McClellan family. All the department has to do is keep it up. We can sit," he said, motioning to a concrete picnic table under a cluster of pine trees, "or we can walk."

"I'd rather walk."

"Then walk it is." He waited for her to start talking. When she didn't, he prodded her. "What was it you wanted to discuss?"

"I think I may have a description of the killer, or at least a description of a possible suspect."

"Keep talking."

CAROLINE RELATED what Trudy had told her. Sam was impressed. He didn't admit it, but she could tell all the same.

"She's scared, Sam, frightened that if this man is the killer, he'll come after her if he thinks she fingered him. I think she could be right, and I don't want to put her in danger."

"Then you can't print this information."

"I never planned to. But you can't go barging into the restaurant asking her questions, either. And you can't leak this so that it gets picked up by some other reporter."

"You're not telling me how to run my investigation, are you, Reporter Lady?" His tone had taken that edge again.

She stopped walking and her hands flew to her hips before she realized she was assuming her fighting stance. "So is this how it is between us, Sam? I'm Caroline if I play the game your way, Reporter Lady if I have an opinion of my own? If I'm frightened and defenseless, you kiss me. If I show any spunk, you knock me down a peg or two, make sure I stay in my place."

He met her gaze. Cold and stony, but there was something else there, a mysterious, haunted quality that she couldn't read.

"I didn't kiss you because you were defenseless. I kissed you because…because…" He turned around and started walking again. "Let's get back to Trudy."

"Fine." But it wasn't fine. She was shaking now, hating that she'd love to throw herself into Sam's arms and forget the killer, forget being a reporter. She was so tired of nothing but talk of murders and fear. But she'd never let herself fall apart that way.

"What about Trudy?" she asked, working to keep her voice steady.

"I'd like to have someone draw a composite from her description of the suspect. Do you think you can get her to cooperate in that?"

"I think so, if we can do it quietly and not let it out to anyone that the description is from her."

"We need to move quickly," he stressed. "The longer we wait, the more likely it is that the man will kill again before we catch him."

"Does that mean you think this could be the guy?"

"It's a lead, and that's more than we had before."

"Is that a Sam Turner version of a thank-you?"

"Yeah, I guess it is." He stopped and leaned against a tree, then caught her hand and pulled her closer. "You did good, Reporter Lady."

His voice had changed, lost its edge and become almost seductive. Of the many faces of Sam Turner, this was the one that blew her away. It was the Sam who'd kissed her last night, the one who made her feel protected and turned her insides to the consistency of rich cream.

Or maybe she was only reading into him the qualities she needed, especially now when she was being drawn into the sticky web of a killer. "There's more, Sam," she whispered. "I heard from him again."

The mood changed in an instant, as if some temporarily benign fury that lived inside Sam had sprung to life. The lines in his face drew tight and his muscles strained against his shirt. "When?"

"Just before I talked to you on the phone. This time he called me on my cell."

He murmured a low string of words he sure hadn't learned from a sainted grandmother. "One day after a murder and he's at it again. The guy just doesn't give up."

"Giving up doesn't seem to be in his plans."

"Did you get a phone number?"

"The handset said unavailable."

"So tell me what was said. Word for word, or at least as best you can remember. Don't leave anything out."

She repeated the conversation. It was if the man's words had been burned into her brain with laser waves.

"He'll call again, Sam."

"But next time we'll be prepared."

"How?"

"We can install a recorder on your cell, office and home phones, for one thing. And a tracking device. All you'll have to do is remember to flick them on the second he starts talking."

"That's not good enough. He'll just say a few words and hang up the way he did today. I have to see him in person."

"Don't start the same trash talk you did the other night, Caroline. We're not dangling you in front of this guy for bait."

"I'm already dangling. He knows everything there is to know about me. He can just pop into my life whenever he wants."

"He's obsessed with you."

"So why not use that to get him?"

"The answer is no. You're not a cop. You're not trained in undercover work. You're not setting yourself up to tempt a vicious killer. End of argument."

"But—"

"There are no buts, Caroline. You try anything that puts you in danger, and I'll lock you behind bars."

"You can't arrest me without grounds."

"Try me."

"So you're just going to wait around doing nothing? Even if Trudy's lead works into an eventual arrest, that will take time. And time can mean another life."

"We're not just waiting around."

"No, you're out here shooting at paper dolls in the middle of the afternoon. What do you call that?"

"Letting off steam so I don't shoot women reporters."

Her pulse skyrocketed in anger. How could she have possibly been even the slightest bit attracted to him? She turned and stormed away, hoping she didn't get lost finding her way back to the car. The last thing she needed was to have to yell for his help.

She didn't have to yell for help, but she obviously didn't go the shortest route. By the time she reached her car, Sam was standing by his with the passenger door open.

"Get in," he ordered.

"You can't tell me what to do, Sam Turner."

"Get in, *please*. And hurry."

"Why should I?"

"I just got a call. There's an emergency on Finnegan Road."

The dread took over again, suffocating to the point it hurt to breathe. "Not Trudy. Please tell me this is not about Trudy."

"She's been in a car wreck."

"She's not…" *Dead.* The word was on the tip of her tongue, but she couldn't say it out loud.

"No, she's not dead. But she rolled the car several times and landed at the bottom of a hill. There's a cop with her now. He's not sure of the extent of her injuries."

"Thanks for waiting for me."

"I had to wait. She's asking for you."

TONY SISTRUNK sat in his office in San Antonio, Texas, mulling over the news that had just landed on his desk and wondering if he should try to get in touch with Sam Turner. He sure didn't want to.

Sam had moved back to Georgia to escape his life here. The news would not only bring it all back, it would piss him off big time. Sam had risked his life to get R. J. Blocker off the streets. Now R.J. was free again, because some appeals judge who didn't know the name of the game much less the score had declared him free on a technicality.

That was the way things worked. Cops risked their lives apprehending the bad guys. Judges came along and ruled it all null and void due to some tiny legal mistake that didn't amount to squat.

R.J. wouldn't come back to a town where he'd killed a cop. Even he wasn't that crazy. But he might be nuts enough to go looking for Sam.

So, as much as he hated to hit Sam with this when he had his hands full with a serial killer, Tony had best warn him that more trouble could be heading his way.

Sometimes life just plain sucked.

Chapter Seven

Caroline climbed into Sam's car, sure that Trudy's crash had not been an accident. Somehow the killer must have found out that Trudy had talked to her and he'd taken action. He couldn't have been in the restaurant. If he had been, Trudy would have known, and as frightened as she was, she'd never have talked to Caroline.

But he could have spies. She thought back to the people who'd been in the Catfish Shack. No one had looked suspicious. But somehow the man had found out Trudy had talked, which meant that the guy Trudy had described must be the killer. She'd point that out to Sam if she ever got the chance.

He was on his phone, giving orders, asking questions, apparently talking to a cop who was already at the scene of the wreck. Caroline half listened, but her mind drifted, and for seemingly no reason she slid back into the cold, dank place that haunted her worst nightmares. The church. The stairs. The feeling that she was being swallowed up by some dark, ravenous creature.

"You okay?"

Sam's voice and his hand on her arm shook Caroline back to the present. She stiffened and turned to face him. "Probably as good as I'm going to get anytime soon."

"The news isn't all bad. Trudy has a head injury. She's lost a lot of blood. Scalp wounds usually bleed heavily, but she's still conscious."

"What caused the wreck?"

"The preliminary indication is that she just lost control and ran off the road."

"The indication is wrong. It's him again, Sam. He knows Trudy talked to me and he tried to kill her, too. The man she described has to be the killer."

"You're jumping to conclusions."

"I'm stating the obvious. Think about it. She talked to me. Within an hour someone ran her off the road and tried to kill her—or at least frighten her into silence."

"We don't know she was run off the road. There are some sharp curves in that road. Take them too fast and you take yourself down the hill."

"Trudy drives the road every day. She wouldn't take them too fast."

"We'll know soon."

"What did she tell the cop on the scene? He surely asked her what happened."

"She said she won't talk to anyone but you."

There were two squad cars at the scene when they arrived, both parked on the shoulder of the road with their flashers on. A gray compact car was lying at the bottom of a steep hill, its four wheels pointing skyward. Trudy was stretched out on the grass a few yards away.

The second Sam stopped the car, Caroline jumped out and took off running, not knowing what she could do to help but desperate to tell Trudy she hadn't betrayed her. When she got there, Trudy was lying deathly still, her hair matted with blood, her eyes closed. The cop who'd been kneeling beside her got up and stepped away.

"The ambulance is on the way."

Caroline knelt by Trudy and took her hand. It was colder than it had been in the restaurant, even though the cop had thrown his jacket over Trudy. A deep gash ran from just above her right ear to the center of her forehead. That appeared to be the worst wound, or at least the bloodiest, but there were other cuts and scratches all over her arms and face, and her right leg was twisted grotesquely, definitely broken.

"Trudy," Caroline said softly, "it's Caroline Kimberly from the newspaper."

Trudy opened her eyes, then closed them again.

"I didn't cause this. You have to trust me."

Trudy gave no indication that she heard her, but Caroline was almost certain she had. "You can just nod if it hurts to talk, Trudy, but I need to know the truth. Did someone run you off the road?"

"Please…"

Trudy's voice was so weak that Caroline had to put her ear to Trudy's mouth. "What is it?"

"Please don't…tell anyone…what I told you about that man."

"It's okay, Trudy. You'll be safe. The police will make sure of that. That beast won't hurt you again."

Trudy groaned and lifted her arm a few inches before letting it drop back to the ground.

"Get my...mother."

"I will, Trudy. I promise. I'll get her right away. Just tell me one thing. Was the man who ran you off the road the one you told me about?"

"I don't know...anything."

The ambulance arrived then and the paramedics rushed toward them. Sam pulled Caroline to her feet. "You tried. That's all you can do."

"I caused this, Sam."

He put a hand on her shoulder. "Get that out of your head right now. Start thinking like that and you won't last a year as a reporter. You've done nothing wrong."

Tell that to Trudy. Caroline started to go to her car, then realized hers was still at the firing range. Her reporter instincts, new as they were, clicked back in, and she watched and scribbled down a few observations while Trudy was lifted into the ambulance.

The killer hadn't wanted Trudy to talk, but why had he run her off the road, instead of cutting her throat the way he had Sally's and Ruby's? That way he could have been certain she wouldn't live to talk. Or had he only meant to frighten her?

And where was he now? Nearby? Watching Trudy being loaded into the ambulance, studying every move the cops made? A cold shudder shot through Caroline. Whether the killer was nearby or not, she knew he wasn't through with her or Trudy yet.

SAM STARTED back up the incline, dead tired and with a throbbing pain over his right temple. This case was taking its toll on his sleep and his health. Brutal, senseless ones like this always did.

To no one's surprise, Caroline had been right on target. This was not a case of simply getting distracted and running the car off the shoulder and down the hill. Skid marks, tire tracks, paint smears and the pattern of dents on the car all indicated that the young woman had been deliberately run off the road. And minutes after she'd given a very sketchy description to Caroline.

And now Caroline was convinced that this was her fault. He had to talk some sense into her before she let the maniac suck her into his deadly scheme. She was innocent and vulnerable enough to believe she could handle him.

And beliefs like that would get her killed.

Sam scanned the area and spotted Caroline leaning against his car, writing in a black notebook. There was blood smeared on the front of her sweater and even some on the side of her face. She didn't seem to notice. She still didn't look tough enough to be a reporter, but she was plucky as hell, that was for sure. And...

He wasn't sure what else, except that she sure had a way of getting to him. Even now when she was standing yards away and paying him no heed. Hair blowing into her face, skirt twisted, sexy boots caked with blood and mud.

And still he couldn't think of anything he'd like to do more than pick her up in his arms and carry her home with him.

"Anything else?" Matt asked, catching up to Sam.

"Did you alert the local cops and state troopers to be on the lookout for a black vehicle with a dented fender smeared with gray paint?"

"Yeah. And I have word going out to all the auto-body shops, as well. If they get anything suspicious in, I told them to call me pronto."

"What about the injured woman's family?"

"We reached Trudy Mitchell's mother, but she'd already gotten the news from the reporter chick. Mrs. Mitchell's at the hospital now."

"Good, and I want a guard at Trudy's hospital door. If this was attempted murder, I don't want the guy to walk in and finish what he started."

"As soon as she's stabilized, they're taking her to an Atlanta hospital."

"Then talk to the Atlanta PD. They've already volunteered any help we need with this case."

"So you're going to let them know you think this could be connected to the two murders?"

"I'd like it kept quiet, but eventually it'll get out. It always does."

"What about the *Times* reporter?" Matt nodded toward Caroline.

"What about her?"

"Do you want me to give her a ride back to her car?"

"No. I'll handle that."

Matt's eyebrows shot up. "You're not falling for the reporter chick, are you?"

"Are you kidding?" Sam answered, avoiding a direct lie. "But she has a name. You can call her Caroline or Ms. Kimberly, if that's not stretching your vocabulary capabilities too much."

"Ouch. So she *is* getting to you. Not your type, though, Sam. Better leave these young, hot ones to an experienced guy like me."

"Any more hot ones, and you'll be burned out before you hit forty."

"Yeah, but what a way to go."

Caroline looked up as Sam approached. "Let's get out of here," he said. "Nothing left now but for Trudy's car to be towed."

"Good. I just need a ride back to my car."

"I thought we could go to my place first, have a cup of coffee and talk. It's practically on the way."

"Your place? I must have heard that wrong. Did I actually hear Detective Sam Turner invite a reporter to his domicile?"

"Yeah, but don't let it get out. It would ruin my reputation."

"Front-page news. Tomorrow's headlines."

"Then I guess I better give you something scandalous to write about."

SAM'S PLACE was only a couple of miles down the road from where Trudy's car had gone off. His house was set back in the trees on the rocky edge of the river. The structure was a mix of cedar and local stone, more like a rustic fishing lodge than a house.

It had two levels, but the first was open and mostly garage and storage for a deep blue bass boat and all the usual paraphernalia fishermen kept on hand.

A rust-red retriever stretched from its nap under a wild plum tree when they approached, then came loping over to meet his master. Sam stopped to rub his hands over the dog and give him a couple of solid pats on the rump.

The dog lapped it up for a second, then turned his attention to Caroline. She stooped and took his head in her hands, running her fingers through the glossy hair on the back of his neck. He licked her hands in appreciation. "*You* are just a sweetheart, you are," she crooned. He nudged his nose between her breasts. "But we don't know each other well enough to get that personal." She looked up at Sam. "What's his name?"

"Brewsky."

"As in beer?"

"Yeah. He wandered up and staked out a corner of my porch one night. Flopped down just like he owned the place. If I hadn't had a few too many beers, I'd never have let him stay."

"That's okay, Brewsky. If the detective decides he doesn't want you, you can come home with me."

Actually a dog wasn't a bad idea, she thought, especially now that she had room for one. She'd always wanted a pet, but they'd been against the rules where she'd grown up.

"Make yourself comfortable," Sam said, gesturing to a den off the front hall as they walked into the house. "I'll put on some coffee and be right back."

"I'd like to freshen up a bit, at least wash my hands and face."

"The bathroom's down the hall. There are clean cloths and towels in the cupboard under the sink."

"Thanks." Caroline found the bathroom and scrubbed the blood from her face. It must have gotten on her when she'd leaned in close to hear Trudy's whisper. She scrubbed her hands, as well, then finger-combed her windblown hair. And that was as good as she could do without a change of clothes.

She returned to the den. It was a man's room, dominated by a cypress-beamed ceiling, dark-paneled walls and massive leather furniture. The combination would have made the room rather dark and forbidding, except that the back wall was almost solid windows with a view of the river and the woods beyond.

The only wall decorations were two huge fish trophies and a stuffed buck's head sporting a full rack of antlers. No knickknacks. Instead, the coffee table was stacked with newspapers and books. And sitting on a shelf was a lone photograph in a silver frame.

Caroline crossed the room for a closer look. The photograph was of a young woman, petite, with striking eyes. The blond hair was shoulder-length, straight and shiny. She had an almost regal nose and sensual lips. The photograph was signed, "Love always, Peg."

Love always, and hers was the only photograph in the room. Caroline wondered if she was still in Sam's life or if she was a past lover—or an ex-wife—he'd never gotten over. It bothered her, but there was no reason to think it was any of her business. Just because Sam had kissed her senseless once didn't mean they had some kind of relationship.

But she wasn't so naive that she didn't know when a man found her attractive. There was a sizzle between her and Sam, even when they argued. And now she was here, in his house for coffee—and talk.

And the truth was she wouldn't be sorry at all if he kissed her again.

In the middle of a crime wave with the killer fixating on her, it would be nice to have someone to hold on to. Not that she'd ever had someone before. Life in an orphanage just didn't work that way. And she couldn't let herself start counting on it now.

WHEN SAM RETURNED to the den with the two cups of coffee, Caroline was standing by the fireplace staring at the photograph of Peg. The irony of the situation was disturbing. Fortunately Caroline didn't ask any questions and he wasn't about to offer any explanations. There was no explaining Peg.

"I like your house," Caroline said, "especially the view. Do you own or rent?"

"It's all mine. I was looking for a place to get away from it all when I moved back to Georgia. This seemed like it. I'll probably keep it as a retreat, but I'm thinking of moving back into town to be closer to the job."

"Do you have family in Georgia?"

"Not anymore, which seemed like reason enough to move back."

"I take it you didn't get along with your family too well."

"You've heard of dysfunctional families? Mine was the prototype."

"But you must have some good memories of family life."

"There were nights my mom and stepdad didn't have a major brawl. I thought that was pretty good back then." Sam didn't know why he was talking about family at all. He usually didn't. But it was so far in the past now that it didn't seem to have the same hold on him, especially with R.J. in prison.

"Did you have brothers and sisters?"

"I had a stepbrother, though I didn't know about him until he was sixteen years old. I was eleven at the time."

"How did that happen?"

"My stepdad was his father. He decided he didn't like responsibility, so he just walked off and left his wife and baby. His wife decided she didn't like responsibility, either, so she walked off and left, too. R.J. was eighteen months old at the time. A little too young to make a living for himself, so the authorities put him in an orphanage in northern Georgia."

"Poor guy."

Caroline's mood seemed to take a nosedive. Why in hell was he talking about this after what she'd been through the past few days? "It's history," he said dismissively, hoping she'd drop the subject. But apparently she wasn't ready to do that.

"Did you and your stepbrother become friends when you finally met?"

"Depends on what you call friends. He used me for a punching bag and ran off all my friends. Used to threaten my mother when she wouldn't give him money for drugs. Which was pretty much all the time because she needed the money to buy her own drugs."

"You weren't kidding about your family being dysfunctional, were you."

"Not a thing I'd kid about."

"What happened to R.J.?"

"He robbed a liquor store one night, not his first, I'm sure. But that night he ran into a little problem. A cop showed up before he could make his getaway. R.J. shot and killed him. Now are you sorry you asked about my family?"

"It is a horror story."

"And that's probably the nicest thing you could say about it."

"Did R.J. go to prison?"

"Yeah. For life. His was my first case after I made homicide detective."

"I'm surprised they gave you a case involving a family member."

"It's a long story." And one that touched on too many other memories for him to handle tonight. "Let's talk about something more pleasant."

The silence between them grew awkward, mainly because they had nothing in common that was pleasant. They'd met at a murder scene, and every meeting since had been entangled with the killer's actions. Everything except the kiss and the awareness level that seemed to soar whenever she was near.

But he had to stay cool and focus on the real reason he'd invited her over today. He had to convince her to keep up her guard at all times and not to even think of trying anything on her own. At least, that was what he'd told himself the reasons were. Now that she was here, his motives were a lot less clear.

He wanted her safe, but he also wanted to reach across the leather couch and pull her into his arms. He wanted to muss her hair and feel her lips on his. He wanted…

He wanted to make love with her and yet he didn't

dare. Relationships were like a foreign language to him. He'd never seen a normal one growing up, and the only one he'd ever been in had happened before he ever thought about it. And when it ended, it had all but destroyed him. He'd had seven years to pick up the pieces, and he wasn't sure they were all picked up yet.

"Talk to me, Sam. I can tell something's on your mind. Just say it."

"I was thinking that you look great in that color."

"No, you weren't. You were thinking something far more serious. Your lips always stretch into thin lines when you're upset."

"You know me too well." He set his cup on the pine coffee table. "You worry me the way you keep thinking that there's something you can do that will keep the killer from striking again."

"He's trying to connect with me, Sam. You can't deny that."

"A dangerous lunatic is obsessed with you. That's not a situation that can be handled by the two of you having a little talk. There's no way of knowing what drives him over the edge. It could be something as simple as a woman resisting his passes—or thinking she can reason with him."

"I promise I won't do anything irresponsible."

"Not good enough. Your idea of irresponsible and mine aren't the same. You think like a reporter. I think like a cop."

"And what if he kills again, Sam? And again? If my meeting with him and talking to him could keep that from happening, then isn't that worth some risk?''

''If he suggests a meeting, then we'll talk about it. But the whole thing will be handled by cops, not by you.''

''You don't think I'm foolish enough to do it any other way, do you?''

''Yeah, I think you might, if he convinces you that seeing him will save someone's life. So promise me you won't do that.''

''Okay, Sam. I promise—at least for now.''

''Good.'' She probably thought he was just being controlling. He was, but he couldn't explain everything to her, couldn't say that knowing she was being stalked by a killer kept throwing him back into his own past and that he simply couldn't deal with that pain again.

The sun was setting, creating patterns of shadows that played on Caroline's face. He ran his arm along the back of the sofa and she slid closer, right into the circle of his arms. She tilted her face toward his.

''I've never had anyone worry about me before. It's not a bad feeling.''

''That's good.'' He wanted to kiss her. He ached to kiss her. He was going to kiss her.

His lips were almost on hers—and then his damn doorbell rang.

Brewsky barked and went running toward the front door. Sam swallowed a curse. Such lousy timing. Normally he could have ignored an uninvited visitor, but not in the middle of a deadly crime wave.

''I'll see who that is and be right back.''

But Caroline didn't wait in the den. He heard her

footsteps behind him as he opened the door. If Matt tried to hide his surprise at finding the two of them together, he did a poor job of it. Sam wasn't about to offer explanations.

"What's up?" Sam asked.

"Police business." Meaning it wasn't for Caroline to hear.

"Excuse us a minute, Caroline," he said, then stepped outside with Matt, closing the door behind him.

"They found a pickup truck that may have collided with Trudy Mitchell's car."

"Where?"

"In the woods off Highway 5. It was set on fire and left to burn. Someone driving by called and reported a stream of black smoke. A state police patrolman checked it out."

"How much damage to the truck?"

"It's pretty much demolished. You should probably get out there."

"Do you mind taking Caroline back to her car? It's at the police driving range."

"I can handle that."

"And make sure she gets home safely."

Matt grinned. "I can handle that, too."

For some reason, Matt's cocky assurance did not ease Sam's mind.

CAROLINE TRIED to concentrate on what Matt was saying, but she couldn't drag her thoughts away from Sam. There was an undeniable and intense attraction between them, but she always had the feeling he was fighting it. If Matt hadn't shown up when he had, they would have ended up in each other's arms. But then Sam would likely have pulled away as he had the other night, leaving her frustrated and wondering what was really going on with him. She had a strong suspicion that the woman in the photograph had something to do with his reluctance to get involved.

Or maybe it was his family history. She'd never thought anything could be worse than having no family at all. Now she wasn't so sure.

"So what does a good-looking reporter like you do when she's not chasing a story?" Matt asked as they turned onto the side road that led to the firing range.

"Not a lot. Mostly I've been busy going through the closets and clearing out the clutter of the old house I'm leasing."

"All work and no play? That's not good for a woman."

"I know. It makes me a dull reporter."

"Maybe you just need the right person to bring some fun into your life."

Oh, no. Not a come-on. Not from Sam's partner. What had she done to deserve this? "I'm not looking for that."

"Are you dating someone special?"

"I don't have time to date these days."

Matt pulled into the gate at the firing range. It was open, though the only car there was hers. "You're not interested in Sam Turner, are you?"

His tone had taken a more serious slant ''
seem to fit the question. "Why do

"I get the feeling something's going on between the two of you."

"What if there were? He's not married..." She stopped, remembering the photograph. "He's not, is he?"

"No, but I don't think falling for the guy would be a good idea."

That was a strange observation coming from the guy's partner. "What's wrong with Sam?"

"Nothing—as a cop."

"But you don't think he's decent date bait?"

"Not for you."

Matt stopped next to her car. It was almost fully dark now. And here she was on a deserted road with a man she barely knew who was saying things that made her uneasy. But he was a cop, for heaven's sake. She couldn't be any safer.

"I'm not planning to get involved with Sam," she said, knowing that at some level she already was. "But if I were, what makes you think he'd be wrong for me?"

"No reason. I just don't think it would work."

"Is Sam involved with someone else?"

"I shouldn't have said anything. Let's just drop this, and I'd appreciate it if you didn't mention this part of our conversation to Sam. He's a nice guy. Take your chances with him if you want."

Just drop it. Why did people always say that after they planted doubts in your mind that you couldn't possibly walk away from? "If you know something about Sam that I should know, just say it, Matt. I'm not good at games. I lose at solitaire, even when I cheat."

"If you're playing solitaire, you really are spending too much time alone."

"Who's Peg?"

"How do you know about her?"

"I saw her picture in Sam's den. Is she someone he's involved with?"

"He was. She's dead, Caroline. Has been for seven years. If you want to know anything else about her, you really should ask Sam. Now, are you going straight home?"

"Why?"

"I'm supposed to make sure you get home safely. Sam's orders. So I'll be the car following right behind yours. I just wanted you to know, so you won't think it's the killer tailing you."

"Thanks." She shuddered as she got out of the car, forgetting Sam as the images of the two bodies that had been found in two different parks crept into her mind. A Prentice police detective would be following her home tonight. She'd be safe, but what about all the other women in town? Would one of them feel the knife of the killer tonight?

A killer that no one could identify except a woman who was too afraid to talk. "I changed my mind, Matt. I won't be going straight home tonight. I'll be stopping at the hospital to see Trudy."

HE FLICKED the ashes from his cigarette out the car window as he watched Caroline climb the steps to the hospital. A cold front had moved in over the past couple of hours, and it was nearing freezing now, but Caroline hadn't bothered to put on a jacket. He imagined her cold nipples pressing against a lacy bra. Her panties were lacy, too. Little thin strips of satiny fabric with exquisite lace that hugged the warm, secret places of her body. He'd seen them hanging across the clothes-drying rack in her backyard just yesterday.

And now she was getting involved with Sam Turner. Sam would be the one to slip his fingers inside the lacy panties she'd hung out to dry. Only, *he* wouldn't let that happen.

Soon, Caroline. Soon it will be just you and me. But first he had to finish what he'd started.

Try to stop me, Sam Turner. Try. But you never will.

Chapter Eight

Caroline was home from the hospital by eight-thirty. The visit had been more distressing than helpful. Trudy had opened her eyes occasionally to stare at the ceiling, but she wasn't talking to anyone. Not even to her mother, who'd sat by her daughter's bed and held her hand the whole time Caroline had been there.

Even with a police guard outside her door, it was clear Trudy was still drowning in fear. So was her mother, though all she officially knew was that someone had run Trudy off the road. Officially that was all anyone knew.

But whether Trudy talked or not, speculation would spread. The town was already crouched in fear, and the fact that any woman had been run off the road in an isolated area would start a new wave of panic and a dozen versions of what had happened, all claimed by someone to be the gospel truth.

Still, Trudy's mother hadn't wanted Trudy moved to Atlanta. In spite of everything that had happened, Mrs. Mitchell felt they were safer close to home. Fortunately Trudy's injuries were far less serious than they'd appeared at the wreck, and the local hospital was adequate for her needs. From a medical standpoint, all she needed was time for the gash on her head to heal and her leg to set.

Caroline sliced a greenhouse tomato for her BLT, then took the sandwich to her small office near the back of the house, stepping quickly as she passed the door that led to the basement. It was silly to be afraid of a harmless draft, especially one with such a logical explanation. The basement wasn't totally underground. There was even a small window visible from the back of the house, but the area was surely colder than the heated upper portion of the house.

One bright and sunny afternoon, Caroline had actually gotten as far as opening the door, but the steep stairs and the dark shadows below had been enough to frighten her so that she'd slammed the door shut and walked away. The fear had nothing to do with the Billingham ghosts or with reality. It was just way too close to the view in her nightmares.

Caroline set the sandwich plate on the table and punched the message button on her answering machine. She had only one phone line to the house and seldom used it for anything except her computer modem, but there were a few people who had the number.

The first call was from Becky, making sure they were still on for the morning and if she minded doubles with a couple of cute guys. Caroline minded. She'd just wanted the physical release of slamming balls across the net, not the challenge of being friendly to some guy she'd never met and would probably never see again. But she'd go along with it. It was easier than explaining to her social butterfly friend why she minded.

The second call was a hang-up. She checked her caller ID. Number unavailable. Damn. It was *him*. She didn't need a message to know that he'd managed to get her home number just as he'd managed to find out everything else about her. It was if he had access to her very soul.

The guy was a dangerous lunatic, but no matter what Sam thought, he wasn't just threatening her, he was reaching out to her. She didn't want to be alone with him, was horrified that he knew where she lived. But he had to be stopped, and unless Trudy talked and gave them a name or a better description, Caroline might be Sam's only link to him. The elusive lead that Sam was looking for.

A man who not only killed but painted bloody X's on women's chests. What did that mean? Why kill both times in a park? Why did the media attention mean so much to him?

All questions without answers. She flicked on the computer screen. She started to type—not newspaper copy, but stream of consciousness, written to the Prentice Park Killer.

Your soul must be black, hideously evil, permanently scarred. What happened to you to make you turn into a beast, instead of a man? And what is it you want from me? Are you crying out for help? Or are you just an extension of my nightmare? Has my past evolved into an unspeakable evil that has been coming my way all my life?

SAM SAT IN THE BOOTH across from Matt. The Grille was all but empty this time of the night except for a few guys at the bar. Matt was swigging down his third beer. Sam was on his first. Off-hours or not, he liked his head clear at times like this—not to mention that he had a killer headache from not getting more than a few hours' sleep a night.

"You think there's a chance they'll be able to get any kind of evidence from the truck?" Matt asked.

"I don't see how they can. Not much left except the shell."

"The guy knew what he was doing, right down to scraping off the vehicle identification number and removing the license plate before he set fire to it."

"Almost as if he thinks like a cop," Sam said.

"Or someone who knows about vehicle identification," Matt added. "How do you think he got back to town after setting fire to the thing? I'd hate to think he has an accomplice, that there are two people that deranged walking the streets of Prentice."

The young waitress stopped back by their table, even though it was obvious they didn't need another beer yet. Service was always great when Matt was around. Young or old, women flocked around the guy. This one was a looker; even Sam had to admit that. Not his type, but a great body and gorgeous hair.

"You guys sure look serious back here," she said.

"Cops are always serious," Matt answered. "You mess around too much with one and you might end up in a pair of handcuffs."

She smiled and trailed a finger down his arm.

"That sounds a little kinky to me, Detective. I guess you have a pair on you, just in case."

"You know, you sound like a babe looking for trouble."

"Well, you know me. I never want more than I can handle, but then I've never had more than I can handle. Want another beer?"

"For starters."

She added a little extra sway to her step as she walked away, and Sam had the feeling there was more than harmless flirting going on. But what Matt did off duty and who he slept with was none of Sam's business, and he didn't really want to know.

"Now that's a hottie," Matt said, finally taking his eyes off her departing derriere. "Not as classy as your reporter, but not bad."

"I don't have a reporter."

"My mistake. I just thought since she was out at your place today that—"

"You thought wrong." Sam wasn't sure why the assumption annoyed him so. Maybe because he wished it was true. But then he'd have to decide what to do about it. It had been seven years since Peg had died. He'd been with women since then, but that was functional. Occasional sex, like an occasional beer. It had never meant much more.

It would be different with Caroline. It was already different.

"It's time you moved on, Sam. You can't live in the past forever."

"Is that what I'm doing?"

"Looks that way to me. I'm sure it looks that way to Caroline, too."

"What does that mean?"

"She saw Peg's picture while she was out there today, still sitting on a shelf like some kind of shrine."

"It's not a shrine. And I'm not living in the past."

"No? She's been dead seven years, yet every time a woman shows any interest in you, you crawl back into the house that Peg built."

"You don't know what you're talking about."

"Caroline's a nice lady. Don't hurt her."

"I don't plan to."

"Yeah." Matt took a long swig of his beer. "So what do we do about Trudy Mitchell? It's damn sure she knows more than she's telling, or the killer wouldn't have gone to so much trouble to keep her quiet."

"There's no proof that she was run off the road by the killer."

"May not be proof enough for a jury, but there's proof enough for me."

"I'm hoping she feels safe enough to talk before he strikes again." Sam finished his drink. He was bone-tired, but a half-dozen pills had dulled the headache. At least, they had until Matt brought up the subject of Peg and what he was going to do about Caroline. Now it was starting up again. "I'm getting outta here," he said. "Gotta get some sleep before the next emergency hits. You coming?"

"Not yet," Matt said. "I'll probably have a couple more beers."

"Keep the handcuffs in your pocket."

"Naturally, partner—until I can put them to very good use."

Sam climbed in his car and headed for his place on the river. But when he stopped at the light, he took a right turn and drove toward the Hunter's Grove area.

He parked half a block down from Caroline's house, but he could see light shining from an upstairs window. Either she was still up or she'd left it on for the ghosts.

He'd love to walk up there, knock on her door and when she opened it, take her in his arms and hold on. But Matt was right. If he wasn't ready to swim, he needed to stay out of the water.

He leaned back and rested his head against the headrest. He should drive home and get some sleep. And he would. But first he had to close his eyes for just a minute. As soon as he did, Caroline danced across his mind, a satin dress twirling about her ankles, her lips soft and inviting.

"I've been waiting on you, Sam. Waiting all my life."

When he opened his eyes again, Caroline's light was out. He started the car and drove home for another almost sleepless night.

"BOY, WAS YOUR GAME on today," Becky said as they headed to the locker room after two hours on the court.

"I needed a physical workout."

"It's those murders. Do you have to write about them every day?"

"It's news."

"Well, I'm hoping the guy's left Prentice and is on the other side of the continent by now."

A nice way of thinking and Caroline wasn't going to burst her bubble.

"What do you think of Dave?" Becky asked.

"He seems nice enough. His tennis is a little rusty. Is he a friend of Jack's?"

"No, he's the new pediatrician in Dad's office. Doctor. Unmarried. New in town so doesn't know any other women."

"Ohhh. So that's why we switched to doubles today. You're matchmaking again."

"That and I wanted you to meet Jack."

"I met him at your party, remember? You're not getting serious about him, are you?"

"I'm not sure. I like him a lot. He's different from the other guys I date. And I get chills when he looks at me with those piercing pale blue eyes. He could just be the one."

"No way," Caroline said, stepping into the changing room and grabbing a towel for the shower. "You are not about to settle down."

"It could happen. You never know when love might hit. So go out there at lunch and bat those gorgeous eyes at Dave, and you can have him sitting up and begging."

"I was thinking of getting a dog for that."

Dave was a nice guy, but it was Sam that Caroline was thinking of when she stepped into the shower. Maybe she should try batting her eyes at him, though the thought of eye batting was pretty disgusting.

He would have kissed her yesterday at his house if Matt hadn't interrupted. She'd instigated the intimacy when she'd moved closer to him on the massive leather couch. She'd wanted his kiss and more.

But if he'd wanted the same, he would have come by last night or at least called. He hadn't, and he hadn't called this morning, either. Maybe a picture in his den and memories were all he needed.

Love always, Peg.

SAM PACED his office Monday morning—if you could call walking in circles around a crowded square office pacing. He had a case that was going nowhere, a chief of police who was on his back night and day, and a frightened citizenry who were walking around with loaded guns.

Trudy Mitchell was still in the hospital, and while the doctors reported she was making a terrific physical recovery, she was still lying there like a deaf mute.

The psychologist they'd called in to consult said it was a result of the trauma and that her speech would probably return soon. Soon could be anytime.

Information tying Trudy to the man who'd killed Sally and Ruby had not been officially released, but speculation was running rampant around the hospital and the town.

No one in Prentice had ever had an armed guard at their hospital door—at least, not in recent memory. And still Trudy didn't feel safe enough to talk. But Sam wasn't giving up.

A good description and a competent artist, and

they'd have the perp's picture out all over the state of Georgia in a matter of minutes. And he knew the artist for the job. All he needed was Trudy to give a halfway adequate description. Something more than the fact that the man was blond and cute.

Sam picked up the phone, surprised that the phone number was right there on the tip of his memory. He dialed the San Antonio Police Department and asked for Captain Tony Sistrunk.

"Speak of the devil," Tony said when Sam identified himself. "I was just reading an article about you and the Prentice Park Killer. Guess you can't get away from lunatics even in rural America."

"Looks that way."

"So how are you doing, you old reprobate? Catching any fish?"

They talked for a few minutes, laughing, remembering old times, leaving a lot more unsaid than said. No mention of Peg. No mention of the guy who'd killed her. The case was cold. No one but Sam probably gave it any thought anymore.

"I was calling about Josephine Sterling. Is she still doing composite sketches for you?"

"Yep. And still the best in the business. Do you have an eyewitness for your killer?"

"I'm not sure." He explained the situation to Tony, including the fact that he might never get his witness to talk. "Do you think Josephine would fly out to Georgia?"

"I'm sure she would. She's a sucker for a challenge."

"Nice to know she hasn't changed."

"Do you want her phone number?"

"Yeah." Sam wrote it down. "Wish you were out here, Tony. You could sink your tobacco-stained old teeth into this case."

"You don't need me. You'll get the guy soon without my help. I don't guess you've heard the latest on R.J."

"I hope it's that my stepbrother is rotting in jail."

"No such luck. The appeals judge let him off on a technicality. Free and clear. Doesn't even have a parole officer."

Sam muttered a few choice words under his breath. "When did that happen?"

"About three weeks ago, but I just found out about it. I tried to call you yesterday, but kept getting a busy signal, and I hated to leave such disgusting news in a recorded message."

"It's only a matter of time until he gets arrested again. The guy's rotten to the core."

"Tell me about it. But he's smart. Never underestimate him."

"Believe me, I wouldn't."

"So tell me about your Prentice Park Killer."

"I could use you here on this one."

Sam and Tony talked for a good half hour, going over the evidence Sam had on the murder cases and discussing possibilities. When he hung up, Sam pulled out the autopsy reports on both victims. He'd read them before, gone over and over them the way he'd done every other bit of information about the murders, but there was always a chance he'd missed something.

Sam's cell phone rang. What now? he thought,

grabbing the phone from the leather pouch at his waist. "Sam Turner."

"Sam, it's Sylvia in records. Did I get you at a bad time?"

"Haven't been a lot of good times for the last two weeks."

"About that reporter, Caroline Kimberly."

"Yeah. I meant to call you. Sorry I forgot. You can forget about checking her out."

"You might not think that when you hear what I found."

His stomach tightened. "Bad news?"

"I'll let you be the judge."

He was shaken when he hung up a few minutes later, even though he knew Caroline's past wasn't really any of his business. Still, knowing it changed things. He'd been in this business too long, knew better than to overlook anything. She was his link with a killer, and now she'd dredged up what might be his only eyewitness, a woman who'd almost gotten killed a short time after she'd talked to Caroline.

He'd trusted everything Caroline had told him, had no reason not to. But he couldn't do that now. For all he knew she could have her own agenda.

He walked to the window and stared out at the parking lot, sick inside, the headache pounding in both temples.

"Hello, Sam."

The voice sent a rush of awareness through him. Like a sip of aged Scotch that burns and feels good both at the same time. He turned and stared much too long. Damn, she looked good.

"What brings you down to police headquarters, Reporter Lady?"

"I need to talk to you."

"Perfect timing. I need to talk to you, too."

"Does it have to do with Trudy? Because I think I might be able to get her to talk if I could see her without her mother in the room."

"No. It has to do with Daphne Greene."

She exhaled sharply, but met his gaze. "What gave you the right to go snooping into my past?"

He motioned to his chair, the only uncluttered place to sit. "Sit down and we'll discuss this rationally."

"No, thank you. I don't sit down with men once they've stabbed me in the back."

He walked over and closed the door. "I had a routine background check done on you. It's my job."

"Routine for suspects. I'm not one."

"You're the only person the killer has contacted. That makes you an integral part of the case."

She turned away and stared out the window. "What did you find out about me, Sam?"

"Evidently you took a fingerprint test when you taught in Atlanta."

"They didn't find anything wrong. They hired me."

"They only checked to make certain you didn't have a criminal record. I had our analyst check further. The prints of Caroline Kimberly matched the prints of a teenager living at the Grace Girls' Home ten years ago. The analyst reported that your real name was Daphne Greene."

"Your analyst was wrong. I was never Daphne Greene any more than I am Caroline Kimberly. I was never anyone. No name. No ties. No relatives. Is that what you wanted to know, that I'm a nobody? Are you happy now, Sam?"

"I'm sorry, Caroline. I just have to ask these questions."

"Fine. Ask away."

"No. I was out of line. You're right, as usual. You're not a suspect and your past is none of my business. But for the record, you're definitely not a nobody."

"You'd have a hard time proving that no matter how many analysts or investigators you had working the case. But you can't just throw out something like this and then back off and say everything's fine, Sam. It doesn't work that way. Ask your questions."

"I don't want to do this."

"Then I'll ask them for you. What happened to your parents, *Reporter Lady?* Who knows? Someone found me in a trash bin in a back alley in downtown Savannah when I was less than twenty-four hours old. Thrown away, buried under coffee grounds and stale food and rancid meat crawling with maggots."

"Did they tell you that in the girls' home?"

"No. I read it for myself in an old newspaper account from the night I was found. I'm nobody, Sam. I got tired of it. So I changed my name and stopped explaining to the world that I was a piece of trash that didn't make it all the way to the dump. I got tired of being me."

There was no bitterness in her voice now, just a distant quality as if she'd faded into some dark place where no one could reach her. The anger had vanished and all that was left was a naive vulnerability, as if she wanted desperately to trust someone but couldn't.

Damn. That was what it was that reminded him of Peg. That look. Haunted. Peg had looked that way when he'd met her on the streets, then later, near the end when she'd been so afraid.

"I left Grace Girls' Home at eighteen," she continued, "and worked my way through college, aided by student loans and a token scholarship. But when I got my first job, I changed my name. I hoped that would put the past behind me. I was wrong. It holds me as surely as if I were bound to it by ropes and chains—by a nightmare."

"But you've come a long way, Caroline. You've accomplished a lot, and you're a damn good reporter."

"Don't suck up to me, Sam. It's not you, especially when I just got a young woman run off the road and seriously injured. And I have a killer who thinks he and I are partners in his sick game of slice and kill."

God, he ached to hold her. But he had no idea how she'd react to that now.

"If you don't have any more questions, I'm going now, Sam."

"Stay. We can go somewhere and talk, get a cup of coffee."

"No, thanks. I have work to do."

"You never said why you came to see me."

"Forget about it. It was probably just a dumb reporter idea, anyway."

"I'm sorry, Caroline. I never meant to hurt you."

"No one ever does. Besides, you were just doing your job, Detective. I'm just one of those reporters who got in your way."

CAROLINE WENT BACK to the office and tried to write up a human-interest article she'd spent the past two days researching—typical behavior patterns of serial killers. Her conclusion was that there were no typical behaviors, though the research itself had been fascinating and terrifying.

Now she just couldn't get into it. She shouldn't have let Sam upset her like that. The surprise was that her name change hadn't come out sooner. No one really got a chance to put their past behind them and start over.

"Boy, do you look down."

"Oh, hi, Ron. I am down."

"Guess that serial killer case is getting to you, huh?"

"It's starting to."

"Murder sells newspapers."

"It appears that way," Caroline said. "John has me doing a column now, a daily update on the progress that's been made. Unfortunately that means I have to stretch nothing to at least eight inches of filler."

"It's too bad about Trudy Mitchell."

"Yes, it is."

"You seem to like her a lot. She must be really nice."

"I do like her. She's young and pretty and scared half to death."

Ron nodded. "I bet, but I hear she's got an armed guard at her door."

"She does for now. She'll be going home soon, and I don't know what'll happen then."

Ron walked away and she went back to her writing. The whole town was talking about Trudy. All speculation, but apparently Ron had heard enough that he believed Trudy's accident was tied to the serial killer. And if he'd figured that out, she was certain a lot of other people in town had figured it out, as well.

It had been five days now since the man had killed his second victim. There had been five days between the first victim and the second. Was five days part of his pattern the way painting in blood was? Was tonight the night he'd kill again?

HE STOOD in the shadows and watched Caroline as she walked out the door of the newspaper office and through the dark parking lot to her car. Five days since he'd killed. Five days since he'd watched the blood rush from a woman's neck as he'd cut her throat.

Strange, but he hadn't expected to enjoy the killing as much as he had. In the beginning it had been just part of the plan. Now it was almost bigger than the plan. The kill itself was taking over his mind.

He couldn't keep it up forever. Sooner or later even a jerk like Sam Turner would get lucky and figure it out. But by then it would be too late. Too late for Sam. Too late for Caroline.

Chapter Nine

The killer didn't strike on the fifth night or on the sixth. Nor had he contacted Caroline again. That was the good news. Sam Turner had not contacted her again, either. And that hurt.

Caroline had thought about their confrontation a lot and come to the conclusion that Sam had been looking for an excuse not to deal with the attraction that sizzled between them. So he'd crawled back into his protective burrow where he could live with his photograph of Peg.

Matt had tried to warn her the night he'd driven her to her car at the firing range. She hadn't wanted to believe him, but he'd been right. So why couldn't she get Sam out of her mind and get on with her life? It certainly wasn't because she didn't have enough other problems to deal with.

John wanted something new and attention-grabbing from her every day, which meant she not only had to cover the routine Prentice news events, she had to find things to write about the two murders. That meant begging interviews from people who deserved their privacy and keeping the murderer on the front page. She was sure the creep loved that.

And on top of everything else, she'd let Becky talk her into meeting at the Bon Appetit for lunch. Now she was here and the place was noisy and packed. But it smelled of cinnamon and nutmeg and baking bread. It was almost worth the trip over for the aromas.

She stepped past a group of women waiting at the hostess desk and scanned the room for Becky. Her friend was standing by a table in the back, talking animatedly to a group of women. Actually, when Becky talked, it was always animatedly. She noticed Caroline and waved her over.

"I saved us a table in the back," Becky said, "so that I don't have to stop and talk to everyone who comes in the door."

"You're doing a booming business. Are you sure you have time to stop and have lunch?"

"Absolutely. I'm the owner."

"If I were the owner, I'd have to be working. I should be, anyway. This will have to be a very quick lunch."

"You, my reporter friend, are turning into a real dud. I'm starting to be sorry I ever told you about the opening at the *Times*. But you are gaining in notoriety."

"Not that I've noticed," Caroline said, sitting down at the table Becky had reserved.

"Then feast your ears on this. I got a call from a guy who writes for some big magazine. He wanted to know the inside scoop on Caroline Kimberly."

"What magazine?"

Becky sat, unfolded her white linen napkin and arranged it over her lap. "I don't remember. It wasn't one I'd heard of before, but it sounded impressive. He's writing an article about you and your work on the Prentice murders."

"When was this?"

"Monday. I meant to call you, but I've been really busy the last couple of days."

"What did you tell him?"

"The truth. That you're smart, vivacious, sexy— and available."

"And you call that the truth?"

"I do. And after that article gets printed, you'll have guys coming to town just to meet you. But give Dave a chance before all these new guys start hitting on you. He really likes you, I can tell."

"Do me a favor, Becky."

"Sure."

"If the guy from the magazine calls again, get his name and number for me, but don't give him any more information about me."

Becky looked stung. "I thought you'd be excited. Publicity is good. I can't imagine why you're upset."

Upset? Try horrified. The man who'd called Becky could be from a magazine. But he could be the killer. Drawn into Becky's life just because she was Caroline's friend. Only, how would he know about Becky?

A smart man can find out anything.

"I'm sorry, Caroline, really. I thought it was a good thing."

"It's not your fault. The killings just have me spooked. But if he calls again, don't talk to him. And definitely don't agree to meet him anywhere. That's very important, Becky.''

''You're frightening me.''

''This just isn't a time to be trusting strangers.''

''Okay,'' Becky said. ''Now I have a little good news.''

''Great. What is it?''

She pulled her left hand from beneath the table and centered it over the unlit candle. The hand was smooth, the nails were neatly manicured and painted bright red and...

''Omigosh!'' Caroline said. ''You're engaged?''

''Yes!''

''When did that happen?''

''Last night. Believe me, I was as surprised as you are.''

''You're engaged to Jack?''

''Yes. What do you think?''

''It's kind of sudden, isn't it?''

''Yes, but he thinks we shouldn't wait.''

''What's the hurry?''

''Jack says if we're in love, we shouldn't wait. We should grab every moment of time we have together and cherish it.''

Caroline had only met Jack a couple of times, but he hadn't seemed the kind of man to utter anything quite that gushy. He hadn't seemed the marrying type, either.

''You don't look very pleased about this,'' Becky said.

''I just didn't know you and Jack were that serious.''

''Sometimes love comes in a heartbeat.''

"Did Jack say that, too?"

"No. I heard that on the biography channel. But it's true. I've always believed in love at first sight. And then I met Jack."

"How long have you known him?"

"A couple of weeks. He came in the restaurant one day for lunch and we hit it off, so I invited him to my birthday party."

"Do you know anything about him?"

"C'mon, Caroline, what's there to know? He's funny and sexy—and his parents have lots of money, so I know he's not marrying me for mine."

"Have you met them?"

"No, but I'm sure I will soon."

"Have you told your parents?"

"Yes. They're skeptical like you, but they'll come around, as long as I'm married in the church. Which I will be. I want a big, perfect wedding. And I want you to be my maid of honor."

"I'm flattered, but you must have a lot closer friends than me. You still see high-school and college friends, and we don't go back nearly that far."

"Sometimes new friends are the best."

"Sometimes." But right now she didn't feel like a friend at all. A friend would tell Becky that she was moving too fast—not that Becky would have listened to her.

They ordered salads and Becky insisted they have a bottle of celebration champagne. Caroline barely touched her salad, which was a mistake, since she drank two full glasses of champagne. Somehow she made it through an hour of listening to Becky talk of wedding plans and how cute Jack was when he popped the question.

She decided it best not to drive, so she took a cab back to the office after Becky exacted a promise that she'd go with her to Atlanta the following week to look at wedding dresses.

It was a promise Caroline hoped she wouldn't have to keep. But maybe she was being too cynical. Love probably was a many-splendored thing when it was right. It was just that it hurt like hell when it was wrong.

Not that she knew firsthand. She was not and never had been in love with anyone, and she was certainly not anywhere near in love with Sam Turner. She wasn't. It was the champagne that was making her miss him so much right now.

"CAROLINE, GET IN here."

She stopped typing and looked up. John was standing at the door to his office, his face red and puckered, a folded newspaper in his hand. Whatever his problem was, it wasn't her fault. He'd approved all her copy before the paper ran.

Still, it was best to humor him when he was in one of these moods. She hit Save, slipped her shoes back on and obeyed his command.

He handed her the paper the second they were behind closed doors. "Care to explain this?"

Her pulse rate soared, and at that moment she could have killed Sam Turner with her bare hands.

"THERE'S A WOMAN here to see you, Sam, and she looks mad."

"Tell her I'm not in."

"Sorry. Someone already told her you were."

"Great. Send her in."

He walked to his desk and stood behind it, steeling himself for whoever would barrel into his office and lay into him because he hadn't caught the infamous Prentice Park Killer yet. It would be the second one today.

But it was Caroline who marched into his office, kicking the door shut behind her. Without saying a word, she crossed the room and slammed a tabloid news magazine down in front of him.

One of the headline articles was circled in red. His eyes went there first and to the picture of Caroline, at the scene of Sally Martin's murder, wearing her slinky red dress. And under it, a caption that read, "Prentice Newspaper Reporter Has Secret Identity."

He scanned the article, his stomach pumping acid. It was all there in black and white. Her name change and ostensible details of her life at Grace Girls' Home, in Meyers Bickham Children's Home and in a foster home before that. All there. Right down to being found in an alley trash bin.

The article also raised questions, suggested that Caroline had been fired from her teaching job and had interfered with the murder investigation by frightening witnesses into keeping quiet about what they'd seen.

If you read between the lines, you might even think she sympathized with the killer, if she wasn't downright in cahoots with him. No wonder Caroline was livid.

"I don't know where they got any of this, but it wasn't from me."

"Then someone in your office leaked it to them. And they wouldn't have had it to leak if you hadn't seen fit to go snooping in my past. You may not have scattered the misguided facts, but you opened the box."

He hated the accusation in her eyes, hated it more because he deserved it. He hadn't meant to pull out her past and shove her nose into it, hadn't meant to hurt her. But he had.

"I don't know what I can say, Caroline, except that I never planned any of this."

"But it doesn't really matter. I'm just a reporter. Say it, Sam. Say I'm just an annoying reporter, a piece of trash that got in your way." Her voice broke. She was shaking, eaten up with anger and hurt.

"I can't say that. It's not true."

A tear rolled down her cheek. Sam swallowed hard, trying to keep some kind of control when her pain was literally tearing him apart. But he couldn't keep control, not when she was crying. He pulled her into his arms.

She beat her fists against his chest, but the tears were coming in torrents now, running down her cheeks and onto his shirt. Finally she quit fighting and just let him hold her while she cried.

When the sobbing stopped, she pulled away. The mood was strained, awkward, confusing. He could have held her forever. That part was easy. It was the talking that was difficult. But he felt he had to say something. The bottom line was that this was all his fault.

"The article doesn't change you, Caroline. You're still the same person you were before it was printed."

"I'll probably lose my job." She looked away as if she couldn't bear to have him in her sight. That hurt, but he understood it. "And I'll have to leave Prentice. Everyone will hate me when they think I've hurt the investigation. I'd thought that living here in the Billingham home would change things. Thought I'd fit in. Make friends. Put down roots."

Her voice was soft, as if the tears had washed away the anger and left only the heartache. "This will blow over," Sam said. "No one puts any stake in what those tabloids say."

"But it's mostly true."

"Not the part that would anger people. You haven't hindered the investigation. You got Trudy to talk."

"And almost got her killed."

"That wasn't your doing."

"Forget it, Sam. I came here prepared to take all my anger and hurt out on you, but I can't. Not when you don't fight back."

"I don't want to fight you, Caroline."

She finally met his gaze, though he couldn't read the intensity in her dark eyes. He only knew they captivated him, made him ache for something elusive and indefinable.

"What do you want, Sam? You kiss me senseless, then never touch me again. You treat me as if I'm a nosy, irritating reporter, have me investigated, then take me in your arms when I explode and hold me while I cry. You're like a groundhog who ventures out of his hole for a glimpse of the sunshine only to scurry back into the darkness every time he feels the heat.''

And he was feeling the heat now. But there was no crawling into a hole, not with Caroline's eyes boring into his. ''I don't deal well with emotional issues.''

''Wow. What a revelation. I'm getting out of here, Sam. I'm not sure I'll be on staff at the *Prentice Times* after today, but if I can help you with Trudy Mitchell, give me a call.''

She didn't allow him time to respond, just picked up her tabloid and marched away. He was tempted to go after her, knew there had to be something he should say, but as usual he didn't have a clue what it was.

He'd love to slam his fist into somebody. The tabloid reporter. The person in the police department who'd leaked the information. A lot of good any of that would do except make him feel better—and get him a lawsuit.

He opened the desk drawer and took out his snapshot of Peg. There was no comfort in it. If anything, he felt she was condemning him, too, telling him he was a coward for not moving on and that it was past time he let her rest in peace.

But mostly the snapshot reminded him that there was a killer out there and that Caroline was still in danger. He'd let a madman get to Peg. He could not let one get to Caroline.

Only, how in hell was he going to stop him?

SAM SPENT the rest of the day at Auburn, interviewing people who'd known Sally Martin before she'd flunked out and returned to Prentice. He'd talked to the ex-boyfriend a couple of days ago. The guy had an airtight alibi that checked out. Even if he hadn't, Sam would have had a difficult time believing he had ever done anything worse than maybe cheat on a calculus exam. Nothing else Sam had discovered raised any red flags, either.

As long as Sam was actively working on the case, he'd managed to keep Caroline on the fringes of his mind. But now he was alone in his car and driving back to Prentice, and she was all he could think about.

She had him figured out. He'd been in his hole ever since Peg had died. It was a long time to live in the darkness, and he wasn't sure he could ever crawl out. And even if he did, he didn't know if he and Caroline could make it together.

Right now, all he knew was that he was a man and she was a woman and he wanted to be with her so badly he could taste it. She might throw him out. That was a chance he'd have to take.

He drove straight to her house, but this time he didn't park half a block away. He parked in front of her house and strode up the walkway. The emotions he wasn't supposed to have were jumping around inside him like a frog in a burlap bag as he rang the bell and waited.

He had no idea what he'd say when she opened the door. He needn't have worried. The knob turned, the door eased open and she stood in front of him dressed in a lacy black teddie that hugged her hips and caressed her breasts. He couldn't have said a word if his life had depended on it.

Chapter Ten

Sam stood in the doorway, desire for her coursing through him. He ached to take Caroline in his arms, carry her off to the bedroom and make love to her. But it wasn't his way and he had no idea what her way was. So he stammered over a hello and then made a stupid cop statement. "Why did you open the door without making sure it was safe first?"

"I made sure. I looked through the peephole."

So she'd known it was him, and she hadn't bothered to throw on a robe. That had to mean something. "I've been thinking about what you said. About my being afraid to crawl out of my hole."

"And did you crawl out, Sam? Is that why you're here? Because I've had a hell of a day, and right now I really need you to hold me and make me feel desirable. If you can't do that, then just leave. I can't possibly take any more talk of killers and stalkers and sick rehashes of every bad thing that's ever happened in my life."

"How could you ever think you aren't desirable? I've wanted to make love to you since that first night when you were prancing around in your red dress and throwing up in the bushes.''

"So don't talk about it, Sam. Just do it.''

And then she was in his arms. He kissed her over and over again. On her lips, her forehead, her long, thick eyelashes, the tip of her nose. And she kissed right back.

He lost all control. Forgot to think or reason. He just wanted to kiss her and touch her and hold her. All of her. His fingers slid beneath the straps of the black teddie. He lifted them and let them fall down her shoulders.

His breath caught and held for one long, excruciating moment, while desire pounded every part of his body. He fought just to keep from falling with her to the floor and ravishing her like some Neanderthal taking his woman.

Somehow he forced himself to go more slowly. He kissed and sucked each nipple in turn, then cradled her beautiful breasts in his hands. She stood there, trembling. At first he thought she was afraid, and he shuddered to think she might change her mind and push him away now that his body was on fire for her.

"Don't stop, Sam. Please, don't stop. I need this. I need you.''

So he slid his hands down the smooth flesh of her abdomen until he brushed across the curly hairs at the apex of her thighs. When he dipped his fingers lower, he discovered that she was hot and wet, ready for him. And he couldn't wait to be inside her, to have her as hungry for him as he was for her.

She wriggled out of the teddie completely, and the

black lace slipped to the floor. Her body glowed in the soft light of the table lamp, and she slipped her arms around him and kissed him, sweet, yet intense. He felt as if she'd reached inside him and touched parts of his soul, bringing it back to life.

Even crazed with desire, he knew that this was more than just sex and that Caroline was offering more than her perfect body. She was offering herself. No pretense. No expectations. Just sweet passion for the taking. If she'd asked for the moon at that minute, he'd have spent his last breath trying to get it for her.

But all she wanted was him.

"Light a fire, Sam."

"Now?"

"Yes. In the drawing room. Everything else in my life is in utter chaos, and I need one perfect memory to hold on to after you've gone."

He wanted to promise that he'd never be gone, that he'd be right here forever, but even out of his mind with desire, he knew he couldn't make that promise. Not yet.

"I'll light the fire. Just don't go away, Caroline. Promise me this isn't a dream and you're not going to disappear on me."

"It is a dream, but I'm not going to disappear."

She led the way to the drawing room. While he built a fire, she threw some big pillows onto the plush Persian rug, then turned on some music. Something classical he'd heard before but couldn't name.

When the first flames danced toward the chimney, he turned around and found her staring at him. "Let me undress you, Sam."

He shuddered in anticipation as she stripped the

shirt from his back, then loosened his belt and unzipped his jeans. The first feeling was sweet relief that the bulge had room to spread, but when she dipped her hands inside his shorts and held him, he knew he couldn't hold back much longer.

He shoved his jeans and shorts over his hips and kicked out of them, then fell to the floor with Caroline in a tangle of arms and legs. She kissed him again, then crawled on top of him and fit her body over his. She moaned when he thrust inside her. He wanted to make it last, but he couldn't. So he just let go. No barriers. No thoughts of anything except sweet, beautiful Caroline.

She came with him, moaning and calling his name as they went over the top.

"Thank you, Sam. That was wonderful. Perfect in every way."

"Oh, Caroline, you really don't know, do you."

"Know what?"

"That the perfection is you."

CAROLINE LAY in Sam's arms long after the lovemaking was through. She didn't want to move, didn't want to break the magical spell that came with sweet fulfillment.

Sam wasn't the first man she'd ever been with, though there hadn't been many. But it was different tonight. For one thing, she'd needed it so badly. When a woman's world fell apart, it was nice to have strong arms hold her tight and have a man make her feel as if she was the most beautiful woman in the world.

But Caroline hadn't needed just any man. She'd

needed Sam. She wouldn't even begin to try to figure out why he affected her the way he did. There probably wasn't an answer for that, anyway. If there was, dating and falling in love would be a science, instead of a magical adventure.

She started to get up, but Sam tightened his hold and pulled her close. "Where do you think you're going?"

"We can't just lie here all night."

"Who made that ridiculous rule?"

She kissed him again, on the mouth so that their breaths mingled and she could taste the salty sweetness of him. "You stay here. I'll go to the kitchen and get us a snack. Do you like cheese and crackers?"

"Not as much as I like what's already in my arms."

"This isn't like you, Sam, saying nice things to a reporter."

"This isn't going in the newspaper, is it?"

"Front page. With pictures."

"Then we should do it again, make sure we get it right," he said. "But you're right." He slid the flat of his hand down her abdomen, looking into her eyes all the while. "This isn't like me. I don't feel like me tonight."

"Is that good?"

"Absolutely, considering I usually feel like I've been wired to explode at any second."

"How do you feel?"

"Satisfied. Indulged. Amazed that you'd want me. What about you?"

"Desirable. Alive." She trailed her lips down his

chest. "And hungry. For something from the kitchen."

"Okay." He opened his arms and released her. "I guess I have to let you eat, as long as you promise to come right back."

"I will."

She left his arms reluctantly, but she was hungry. It was a good sign. She hadn't eaten anything but the few bites of salad at Bon Appetit all day. And then John had hit her with the tabloid.

Her problems weren't over. Making love with Sam couldn't solve everything. She'd probably still lose her job. And the killer was still out there. He could be stalking her tonight, might even know that she was with Sam. Or he might be out with his next victim.

A shiver rode her spine as she sliced the cheese. Neither she nor Sam had mentioned the killings tonight, but she knew they were never far from Sam's mind. Still, the lovemaking had been incredible.

They hadn't talked of feelings or commitment. She knew he wasn't ready for that yet, but he'd been here for her, made her feel loved when she'd never felt more like the trash her parents had believed her to be. No matter what happened between her and Sam, no matter what the rest of her life was like, tonight would live in her memory forever, one glowing moment to counteract the secrets that hid in the dark crevices of her mind.

But she wanted more. She wanted Sam again—tonight. She was already feeling the surge of desire by the time she got back to the drawing room with the cheese and crackers. But not Sam. He was lying on his back, his head falling off one pillow, his arm thrown across the other—and he was snoring softly.

She sighed and poked a cheese-laden cracker into her mouth. The first time she'd had a man stay over since she'd moved into the house, and he was sleeping.

Taking the chenille throw from the couch, she spread it over his naked body. She started to go back to her bedroom, but changed her mind. Her world might be falling apart at the seams, but she'd sleep in Sam's arms tonight.

SAM AWOKE from the soundest sleep he'd had in years to the smell of bacon and coffee. He stretched and looked around, confused for a minute about where he was. But when he slipped from under the light throw and saw his naked body, it all came back to him, accompanied by a quick stirring in the groin.

And a bit of apprehension.

The memory rushed back into his head, hitting him with a new wave of desire. Last night had been perfect. Being with Caroline had been perfect. But now it was morning.

Time for the next step in the relationship dance, but he wasn't sure what that should be. Fast or slow or somewhere in between. And even if he knew what the step was supposed to be, he wasn't sure he could make it.

He stretched and looked around for his pants. They were draped neatly across the back of the sofa. He was certain he hadn't put them there. His mind went back to Caroline as he pulled on the jeans and zipped them. He didn't bother to close the snap. He needed coffee. Needed it bad.

He needed it worse when he caught sight of Caroline. She wasn't naked anymore, but she was wearing a frothy little purple cover-up that stopped short of her knees. Her feet were bare, and her toenails were painted a shimmering pink.

He didn't know what she was cooking, but she looked good enough to eat.

"Good morning, Detective. I wasn't sure if I should wake you or let you sleep."

"What time is it?"

"Seven-thirty. I'm an early riser."

"I normally am, too. I usually wake up a dozen times during the night—the nights I actually get to sleep."

"Hmm. And you slept all night long when you were with me. Doesn't say too much for the excitement level I generate."

"Guess you'll have to work at keeping me better entertained," he said, tying to keep the mood light, though he knew he wasn't doing a great job of it. One part of him wanted to take her in his arms and make love to her again. The other part was on the verge of turning tail and running. Neither seemed appropriate.

"How do you like your eggs?" she asked.

"Over easy, if it's not too much trouble."

"No trouble at all. Coffee's in the pot. There's a mug on the counter. Help yourself."

He did, then leaned against the counter and watched her break two eggs and slide them into a layer of hot grease. Bacon and eggs cooking. Her in her froth. Him in his jeans and no shirt. Both of them barefoot. Like lovers.

"I've been thinking about the killer's MO, Sam."

End of the lover routine. Back to the macabre. He hated this for her. Murder was his job, but she'd been thrown into it without even getting a chance to prepare for it—not only as a reporter, but as a target of a stalker. "What about his MO?"

"The way he smears blood on the breasts as if he's X-ing them out. I think that could be his way of striking back at his mother. I mean, you suckle at the breast when you're a baby. It's the first bond."

"So you think he wasn't nurtured."

"He could have been deserted the way I was, or maybe abused. At any rate, maybe he hates the idea of motherhood. I know I'm not any kind of expert at this, but that's the way I see it."

"You make a good point."

"And the other thing I keep thinking about is the way he never seems to get caught. He shows up here with a cookie. He leaves a note on my car. He follows me to the Catfish Shack, or at least knows I've been there. But no one ever notices anyone hanging around who doesn't fit in."

"I know. It's almost like he's invisible," Sam agreed.

"Could he be a cop or an ex-cop? Or at least someone who's been in the military or some area of law enforcement? He seems to know too much about getting information to be just an ordinary citizen."

"Maybe you should train as a profiler. You sound exactly like one."

"I'm just trying to make sense of this."

"I know. I've gone over the same things you have, but all we have are assumptions that don't lead to a suspect. It's not unusual for serial killers to be hard to apprehend, though. If they weren't, they'd get arrested before they became serial killers.

"But the main reason most of them are so elusive is that they choose their victims randomly. Since they have no connection to the victim before the murder, there's no way to know they're suspects, not even in a town like Prentice where everyone knows everyone else and most of their business."

"Maybe he's not from Prentice."

"That's my guess," Sam said. "But that's still an assumption. We need something solid."

"I'd like to see Trudy again," Caroline said. "I may stop by the hospital this afternoon. I'm meeting my friend Becky for lunch. She's worried about me and feels a little guilty, I think."

"Why would she feel guilty?"

"She most likely provided some of the information about me that was in the tabloid article. Not meaning to, of course. She thought she was talking to a legitimate magazine that wanted to give me positive attention. Needless to say, they twisted every word she said."

It was the first mention of the article since she'd left his office yesterday, but they couldn't keep avoiding it. Caroline served the eggs, along with bacon and crisp whole-wheat toast. They kept talking while they ate, the awkwardness disappearing as they spoke.

"What's up with the job?" Sam asked. "Are you going to get fired over those ridiculous tabloid insinuations that you interfered with the case, or is your boss going to be reasonable?''

"I'll find out this morning. I'm meeting with John at ten. He wanted time to consider the situation and its impact on the newspaper before he made a final decision."

"He'd be a fool to let you go."

"I was a grunt reporter until a couple of weeks ago. I'm sure he doesn't think I'm irreplaceable."

"What's a grunt reporter?"

"Someone who does the boring stuff, the articles the more experienced reporters don't want to bother with."

Sam's phone rang. Probably Matt wondering why he wasn't already at the precinct—he usually was by this time of the morning. He excused himself and made a run to the drawing room to catch it before it stopped ringing.

"Detective Sam Turner."

The caller wasn't Matt. It was someone at the hospital. There'd been a change in Trudy Mitchell's condition. She'd said she wanted to talk.

He went back to the kitchen and gave Caroline the news. She was in this deep enough to deserve to know.

"I'm going with you to the hospital, Sam."

"As a reporter."

"As Trudy's friend. And because I want the killer caught."

"Can you be ready in ten minutes?"

"You know it."

She was ready in eight. No froth and no makeup, but she was the same spunky Caroline he was used to. The woman she'd been before the tabloid had shot a hole the size of Georgia in her self-confidence and brought back all the painful memories from her past. He knew she wasn't past it all, but she was coping again, and she'd get there in time.

Now if Trudy had only recovered that well.

TRUDY WAS SITTING UP in bed drinking a glass of orange juice when they walked into the hospital room. Her hair was combed and she was wearing light makeup. Even the hospital gown had been exchanged for a blue-printed pajama top and a pair of loose shorts, stretchy enough to fit over the cast on her right leg.

"Hi, Trudy," Caroline said. "You look great."

"I'm better."

"Looks like you're taking good care of the patient," Sam said to Mrs. Mitchell.

"I'm doing my best. My daughter's a remarkable young woman."

"That she is," Sam agreed.

"I'm lucky to be alive," Trudy said. "Luckier than Sally or that other girl who was killed."

"Yes, you are." Sam stepped to the edge of the hospital bed. "We need to find the guy who killed them."

"I know." Trudy turned to her mother. "I have to tell them what I know, Mom. If I don't, he's going to kill someone else."

Mrs. Mitchell's face twitched repeatedly just above her left eye. It didn't stop twitching until she'd moved to the side of Trudy's bed and placed a hand on her arm. "You know how I feel about this."

"I know you want to protect me. I want that, too, but I have to do this."

"Trudy's protection will be top priority, Mrs. Mitchell," Sam assured her. "We'll make sure she's safe until this guy is behind bars."

"Yes, the way the police protected Sally and Ruby." Mrs. Mitchell clutched the bedside railing so hard that her knuckles turned white and the blue veins on the back of her hands stood out like ropes.

She turned to Caroline. "This is all your fault. You got my daughter into this just like the article said. Now you get her out. Tell her she doesn't have to talk. Tell her this isn't her duty."

Caroline swallowed hard. She understood Mrs. Mitchell's agony, was even, in fact, amazed by it. Some mothers *did* love their daughters so much that they'd do anything to keep them safe. It was nice to know.

Still, they needed Trudy to talk. Other lives could depend on it. But then, how could she push her when she had no way of knowing if Sam could make good on his promise? The killer still seemed to hold all the aces.

"Trudy's very brave, Mrs. Mitchell," Caroline said. "You should be proud of her for having the courage to do what she thinks is right."

"It'll be okay, Mom," Trudy said. "You'll see. It will be okay."

Mrs. Mitchell ran the back of her hand across her eyes, catching the tear that had wet her lashes. "I'd like to be here while you tell them what you know."

"We've already talked about this, Mom. It's better for me if you're not."

"Okay. I don't understand why you can't say what you have to say with me in the room, but I'll be outside if you need me."

Trudy reached out her hand and her mother took it.

"I love you, Mom."

Mrs. Mitchell bent and kissed her daughter on the cheek. "Love you, too, sweetie. Love you, too."

Mrs. Mitchell didn't look at Caroline or Sam as she left the room. In her mind, doubtless, they were the villains who were dragging her daughter into danger. Sam wouldn't buy that. He'd make certain the police kept Trudy safe. It was a cop thing.

Caroline had her doubts. Hope for the best but always be prepared for the worst. It was an orphan thing.

TRUDY WATCHED her mother leave. She hated to disappoint her. She'd felt the same way at first. She'd been so scared when her car had started rolling, not so much because she'd die in the car wreck, but because she wouldn't—and the guy would come racing down the hill and pull her from the car.

She imagined him ripping off her clothes and slicing her throat wide open with a knife, as he'd done to Sally and Ruby. Only, he'd be even meaner to her because he thought she'd squealed on him. Sally had thought he was great. Trudy knew differently and her heart constricted at the memory. The things she'd never told anyone. The things they'd done.

"Are you ready to give us a description?" Sam Turner asked.

"I can do better than that. I'll give you a name."

Chapter Eleven

Trudy pushed herself up straighter in the hospital bed. "I'm sorry I didn't tell you this at first, Miss Kimberly, but I was afraid."

Her voice had dropped to a whisper as if she thought the man she was about to name might be close enough to hear. Caroline understood that fear.

"What's his name, Trudy?" Sam asked.

"Billy Smith."

Sam stepped closer to Trudy's bed. "Was Sally dating Billy?"

"No. I told the truth about that part. He wanted her to go out with him. He hung out in the bar two or three days a week."

"Did she like him?"

"Not at first, but he kept after her. They'd started talking a lot. And then…"

Trudy started shaking and taking quick, choppy breaths.

Caroline had moved over by the window, trying not to interfere with the questioning, but now she rushed to the bed and put a hand on Trudy's shoulder. "Do you need a nurse?"

"No." Trudy took a series of deep breaths. "I'm okay."

Sam poured a glass of water and handed it to Trudy. "Take your time, Trudy. No rush. You're doing just fine."

Trudy nodded, but she drank every drop of the water before she started talking again. "I saw Sally and Billy outside one night when she took her break. They were kissing and he was feeling her up. Had his hand under her sweater."

"Did she seem upset that he was touching her?"

"No. And then when they came back inside they were laughing and whispering to each other. I think she might have left with him that night, but I don't know for certain."

"Was that the night she was killed?"

"No. It was the Tuesday before she was killed."

"Do you know if she had a date with him the night she was killed?"

"She came to work that afternoon, but then she got a phone call. A few minutes after that, she said she was sick and left early. But she hadn't seemed sick before she got the call. I think she went to meet him and then he killed her."

"What else do you know about Billy Smith?"

Trudy hesitated, then knotted her hands in the white sheet. "He's bad, Detective. Mean. And he hurts women."

"How do you know that?"

"Because he used to come in and flirt with me. That was before Sally came to work at the Catfish Shack. He hung around me, just like he did Sally. Flirting and trying to get me to go out with him."

"Did you?"

She turned away, then put her hands to her face. When she moved her hands, Caroline could see the tears welling up in her eyes. "I went out to his car with him one night."

"What happened?"

"We were supposed to go for a drive, but we only went a little ways along a road behind the restaurant. Then he just pulled the car into the trees. I was nervous, but everything seemed all right at first. We were just kissing, playing around. Not doing anything wrong, though my mother would think it was."

And Caroline had an idea Mrs. Mitchell hadn't heard this part of the story—which explained why Trudy didn't want her in the room during the questioning.

"So what makes you say he's mean?"

Trudy pushed her fingers through her hair and shoved it behind her ears. "He had some whiskey with him. I took a couple of sips, but he was drinking a lot. Then he started putting his hands everywhere but...he was rough. I told him he was hurting me, but he just got rougher."

"What did you do?"

"I begged him to stop. He wouldn't. No matter what I said, he wouldn't stop. He said it was what I wanted, that I'd asked for it."

"Did he rape you?"

"He tried to, but I got a knee into his groin. He yelped real loud, then shoved me out of the car and drove off. I walked back to the restaurant in the dark. It was scary, but I didn't care. Even knowing there's snakes out there wasn't as bad as being with him."

"Did you report this to the police?"

"No. I was too embarrassed. Besides, who'd believe it was attempted rape? I was drinking and necking on a lonely road. The next day he came by and said if I ever told anyone what had happened that night, he'd kill me. And the way he said it, I believed him. I still do."

"Have you talked to him since Sally was killed?"

"He came in the next afternoon. I was working behind the bar. He waited until no one else was around and then told me again that he'd kill me if I mentioned anything about him and Sally to the police. And…and then he tried to by running me off the road and down that hill."

"He's not going to kill you," Sam said confidently. "Do you know where this guy lives?"

"Well, he told me he lived in Grantville, but he told Sally he lived in LaGrange, so I guess he was lying."

"What about the description you gave me?" Caroline asked. "Was that accurate?"

"Yeah. I told the truth about that. I don't know how he found out I talked to you, but he did."

"Or else he just figured you would break eventually," Sam said. "He might have already planned to run you off the road as a way to make you even more afraid. It could have been coincidence that it happened the same day you talked to Ms. Kimberly."

"Did you see him that day, Trudy?" Caroline asked. "Do you know for sure that it was Billy who rammed your car?"

"I didn't see his face. I was too scared and too

busy trying to keep the car on the road. But it was deliberate, and who else would do such a thing?''

She repeated her description of Billy for Sam while Caroline tried to paint a visual picture in her mind. Blond hair. Tanned. Average height. Average build. No distinguishing marks. Well dressed. Smooth talker.

Sam made a few notes, then rubbed his whisker-studded chin with his hand as if he was still trying to figure all this out. ''What kind of vehicle does he drive?''

''Usually he was in a red sports car, but he was driving a black pickup truck the day he ran me off the road. Guess he didn't want to mess up his car just to kill me.''

Sam asked a few more questions, but it appeared that Trudy had either told all she knew or she was sliding back into her fear zone.

''We're going to get out of here now,'' Sam said, ''and let you rest, but I want you to keep thinking about what you told us. If you remember anything else, give me a call.''

''I will.''

Caroline took Trudy's hand and squeezed it. ''You're very brave.''

''Thanks.''

''But what happened to change your mind about talking to us?''

''It was that article about you, the one where they said you were an orphan and that your mother had thrown you in a trash can. They made it sound like you were dishonest for changing your name, but I don't agree. And I just figured if you can be out there trying to help find Sally's killer when you've had such a hard life, I should do my part. I mean, I have great parents who love me and they're going to stand by me no matter what.''

So the article Caroline loathed had actually accomplished something worthwhile. It might even lead them to the Prentice Park Killer. There was no way of knowing when a break would come.

CAROLINE WISHED she could go home and spend a little more time on her appearance before going to her meeting with John, but she couldn't be late. In the morning rush, she hadn't had time to shampoo her hair or apply makeup, but she'd have to do.

Sam had been just as rushed. He'd forgotten his wallet at her house. Fortunately she'd had an extra key, the emergency one she kept in the car. She'd let him take it.

She exceeded the speed limit more than once and made it to the office with three full minutes to spare. On time for the final verdict. She'd love to tell John that the article might be instrumental in capturing the serial killer, but then he'd insist she print the whole story about Trudy, and she wasn't going to do that until the killer was apprehended and she knew Trudy was safe.

A reporter with scruples. She was living proof that they did exist. She rushed in and went straight to John's office.

''If you're looking for John, he's not here,'' Ron said.

''Where did he go?''

"He didn't say, but I saw him get in his car and drive away about an hour ago."

"Thanks."

A reprieve, but it irritated her, especially after the way she'd rushed to keep their appointment. It puzzled her, as well. It wasn't like John to miss an appointment.

She went back to her desk, but she was in no mood to work—not until she knew whether or not she had a job.

Too nervous to just twiddle her thumbs while she waited, she took out the notes she'd taken about Billy's appearance. Blond hair, tanned body, smooth talker, sharp dresser. Not very specific. Not enough to convey a good visual image.

She doodled on piece of scrap paper, then picked up a clean sheet of printer paper and started sketching a man. If Trudy had been able to describe the shape of the head, it would have been a lot easier, but since she hadn't, Caroline started with an elongated egg shape. Eyes close together. Trudy hadn't said that, but when Caroline pictured someone evil, she always imagined the eyes close together, and bushy brows.

But that wouldn't fit with the "nice-looking" comment Trudy had made about the guy back at the restaurant. So Caroline changed the eyes and erased part of the brows. The ears and nose would likely be nondescript. If they'd been large or misshapen, Trudy would have noticed. So Caroline drew them in, all average, and added a mouth. Kind of thin. Not sure where that came from.

"What you drawing there, Caroline? The man of your dreams?"

She looked up. Ron was standing there, holding a stack of folded newspapers and a cup of steaming coffee.

"Definitely not the man of my dreams," she said.

"I saw that article about you in that gossip magazine. You ought to sue them for slander."

"I thought about it, but they'd just chew up and spit out any attorney I can afford."

"I heard that John was foaming at the mouth."

"I'm not even sure I'll still have a job after today." She probably shouldn't be saying that around the newspaper office, but if Ron knew about it, she was certain everyone else did, too.

"He won't fire you. Controversy sells more papers than complacency. The phone's been ringing all morning in circulation. Everyone wants to read your accounts of the murders just to see what all the fuss is about."

"I hope you're right."

"I was surprised to hear you once lived in Meyers Bickham."

"Had you heard of the place?"

"I had a friend who was there for a while when he was a kid. He says if you lived through Meyers Bickham, you can live through anything."

"I lived there less than a year. I don't even remember the place. I guess it's probably been torn down by now."

"Naw, it's still there. Condemned, though. I imagine they'll tear it down soon. Just an old church with a bunch of busted windows. You can't even tell it was ever a home for kids whose mamas ran out on 'em.''

A church. Steep, dark stairs. The images from her recurring nightmare crept through her mind, and as always she felt a cold shiver of fear. ''I didn't realize it had ever been a church.''

''Oh, yeah. Had a tall spire and everything. Mostly my friend remembered the rats. Big, gray ones. He's grown now and still scared to death of rats.''

Caroline shuddered. ''Me, too. Horrified even by mice.''

''I'm sorry. I didn't mean to upset you.''

''I'm fine.'' She looked up at the sound of voices outside her cubicle. John had returned.

''I guess I better get back to work,'' Ron said. ''John wants me to check the dispensers often today and refill them when they sell out. You're a hot item, Daphne.''

''Caroline. Daphne no longer exists.''

''Whatever.'' He took another look at her drawing. ''That guy looks familiar.''

''Really? Where have you seen him before?''

''I don't know, but he looks familiar.''

That spooked her. The killer could have been here, and it was possible Ron had seen him. Just an average-looking guy, kind of cute. But cruel. He liked to hurt women. And to kill them.

She couldn't think about this anymore now. She had to see John and find out if she was going to eat next month and still have her marvelous old house to sleep in. Besides, Sam had a name. The Prentice Park Killer would likely be in jail by dark.

CAROLINE WALKED into the Prentice Country Club
dining room at ten minutes after twelve. The crowd
was sparse. There was a group of about twelve
women at three round tables in the back, mostly
gray-haired. Caroline recognized some of them from
the articles she'd done when she was covering social
events. A life she could barely remember at this
point, though it was only three weeks past.

The rest of the group was a mixture of women in
tennis attire, men in their golf slacks and polo shirts,
and a few tables of men and women in business suits.
The country club was casual during the day and
weeknights, but turned semiformal on Friday and
Saturday nights.

It wasn't the kind of snooty atmosphere you got
in an exclusive club in a big city, but for a rural
Georgia town, it was about as classy as you'd find.
Becky fit in like cracked pepper on pizza—spicy, but
needed to liven up the place. Caroline didn't fit in at
all. Becky never seemed to notice.

She waved at Caroline from a table near the back
window. There was a bottle of champagne chilling
in a bucket next to her. Caroline dodged a waiter
carrying a tray of salads and joined her friend.

"More champagne? This isn't another celebration,
is it?"

"Could be. How did it go with John?"

"'Well, after giving this careful consideration,'"
she said, mimicking John's serious tone, "'and after
talking to the chief of police and getting a last-minute
phone call from Detective Sam Turner…'"

Becky did a quiet drum roll by smacking the back

of her spoon against a folded napkin. Caroline laughed.

"John agrees that the tabloid blew everything out of proportion and that since I am doing a good job, there's no reason to let me go."

"*Good?* How about you're doing an *excellent* job? I had all my friends call the circulation department this morning and arrange to subscribe so that they could read the coverage by Caroline Kimberly."

"That explains the action in circulation. But does that mean none of your friends took the paper before?"

"Not many. We're the Internet-news generation. Newspapers are too slow. But you kept your job. That calls for champagne." Becky motioned for the waiter, who came, white towel folded over his arm and ready to pour. They clinked glasses. "To your job," Becky toasted.

"And paying my bills."

"Now I have a little good news," Becky said.

"You postponed the wedding."

"Bite your tongue! This is top, top secret, so you can't breathe a word—not until it's all said and done."

"So give. What's up?"

"Jack and I are eloping."

"When?"

"I can't tell you, but soon."

"But just yesterday you were planning a big wedding. You asked me to be your maid of honor."

"I know, but we just can't wait."

"Oh, Becky, I know you're infatuated with Jack,

but it's so quick. How can you be sure it's love or that Jack's even being honest with you?''

Becky reached over and put her hand on Caroline's. ''When you fall in love, you'll understand. Be happy for me, Caroline.''

She wanted to be. She really did, but she had this ominous feeling in the pit of her stomach. Maybe it was the murders and Trudy and all the terrible things she dealt with day after day, but it frightened her that Becky was jumping in so deep with a guy she barely knew.

But she'd said all she could. When they finished lunch, she left quickly. She couldn't fake enthusiasm for the wedding, and she really did have work to do.

She spent the afternoon in the mayor's office, then rushed back to the newspaper to write up an article on his proposal for bringing more tourists to town for the annual spring pilgrimage. The pilgrimage was one of her favorite events, but this afternoon her mind kept going back to Becky—and to Sam.

Love. Strange that Becky was so sure of it when Caroline found it so daunting and undefinable. Something definitely existed between Sam and her. He'd been on her mind almost constantly since she'd met him. Even when she was angry with him, the chemistry between them was so strong she couldn't think straight.

But even after making love, she had no idea where she stood with him. He hadn't said a word about his feelings toward her. And he hadn't mentioned seeing her again. If it was up to her, he'd be back tonight, and tomorrow night and the night after that. She wanted to feel his lips on hers. Wanted to lie in his arms with her naked body pressed against his. Wanted him inside her.

Her body grew warm. She finished the article and shut off her computer. Everything else she had to do could wait until tomorrow.

She started to call Sam, then changed her mind. She didn't want to seem desperate to see him. And even if she just called to ask how the search for Billy Smith was going, he might think she was putting him on the spot—or that she was pushing the edges of their personal relationship to get information for a story.

If he missed her, if he wanted to see her tonight, he'd call. And if he didn't...

Love always, Peg.

GEORGIA WAS OVERFLOWING with males named Billy Smith. All ages. All colors. All religions. All socioeconomic groups. And any number of occupations. But there were no Billy Smiths in La Grange or in Grantville, at least none anywhere near the right age to be the guy they were looking for. So the guy was not only a rapist and possibly a killer, he was a liar. No surprise.

"Man, this is frustrating," Matt said, groaning and stretching his neck. "We finally get a decent lead, and it bogs down in sheer numbers."

"We need more. I need DNA or prints, something I can match up with FBI and Georgia criminal records. Or I need a picture of the guy."

"Didn't you say you know of a super-talented composite-sketch artist in San Antonio?"

"Yeah. I'm going to try to get in touch with her

tonight. I'd like to have her fly up and talk to Trudy tomorrow. If anyone can get an image from Trudy's mind to a piece of paper, it's Josephine.''

"At least it's not a full moon tonight," Matt said.

"There wasn't a full moon the night Ruby was killed."

"You're right, and full moon or not, I have this crazy premonition that he's going to strike again real soon."

"That's called instinct," Sam said.

"Are you thinking the same thing?"

"Yeah. He likes a media circus with all three rings going, and his hold on the news and talk shows is slipping. The president beat him out for top billing on Channel Six tonight."

Matt heaved a sigh. "And of course, it's likely the guy lied about his name. He could be anybody from anywhere."

"Anybody from anywhere with a sharp knife and a habit of applying it to women's throats." Sam was thinking out loud more than making conversation. Mostly he was thinking about Caroline and the killer's penchant for letting her know he was watching her. If the tabloids had known about that, they'd have had an even bigger field day. And might have sent the guy completely over the edge.

"Are you working until all hours again tonight, partner?" Matt asked.

"I'll work awhile longer. I guess you've got a hot date."

"Medium hot. But promising. What about you? Are you seeing your reporter lady?"

"I don't have a reporter lady." But in spite of his

statement, he could see Caroline even now. In her black teddie, looking up at him with those big brown eyes. Damn. This wasn't going to work. He should stay away from her altogether. He was no good for her.

He waited until Matt left, then pulled the picture of Peg from the drawer. "I let you down. I promised to get your killer, but I didn't. It was the least I could have done."

He'd loved her so much. But she was gone. Now if only the guilt would die, as well.

CAROLINE PARKED her car in the garage, grabbed her briefcase from the seat beside her and climbed out of the car. The worst thing about winter was coming home when it was already dark. She liked to spend time outdoors, puttering in the garden or sometimes taking long walks through the neighborhood.

The old houses intrigued her. They had so much more personality than the ones that seemed to spring up overnight in the newer subdivisions. All with history. All with roots. Her roots were in a trash can and stored at Meyers Bickham.

An old church. A dark basement. Big gray rats. It sounded far more like the setting for a horror movie than a state-run facility for children no one wanted. When this was over, she might visit the place and see if she could put her nightmares to rest. It was bound to look different to her now than it had when she was seven.

But right now she had living nightmares to deal with.

She started toward her back door, then stopped.

The top had blown off her garbage can again. Fortunately the new outdoor lights Sam had insisted she put in illuminated the area well. She picked up the lid and fit it back on the plastic bin. Something moved in the bushes just outside the ring of light.

Her heart jumped to her throat, then settled back in a chest that seemed too tight to hold it.

It was only the wind.

Once inside, Caroline made herself a salad and ate it at the kitchen table she'd bought at a thrift store. The same table where she and Sam had eaten breakfast this morning. And where she'd sliced cheese last night after they'd made love.

She picked up her plate and took it to the small office at the back of the house, where she turned on her computer. She would not waste an evening thinking about Sam or fretting over whether he'd call.

Setting her half-eaten salad on the edge of her desk, she logged on to the Internet and checked her e-mail. Twenty-five new messages. She wasn't up to wading through them.

Almost without thinking, she typed ''Meyers Bickham'' and hit Search. She doubted she'd find anything, but now that she knew she'd lived there for a while, she'd like to know something more about the place.

She scanned the list of entries and soon found what she was looking for: Meyers Bickham Children's Home. The link was to an article written in 1994. She double clicked and went to the site.

In the Shadow of the Spire

A strange title for an article about an orphanage, but Meyers Bickham was mentioned in the opening sentence. She read the piece quickly, then went back and read it again as the familiar but nebulous fears swept through her.

The orphanage had been housed in a converted church on a Georgian hillside. To an outsider, it was a place where children ran and played in the sunshine, but to the children who lived there, it was a place of endless rules and harsh punishment for those who broke them. A place where laughter was rare, winter nights were cold and dark, and the nighttime lullaby was the scratching of rats inside the crumbling walls.

The article had been written just after the orphanage had closed its doors for good. The author claimed it was based on his memories of the two years he'd spent there, but then, authors tended to use a little creative license even in nonfiction. Surely the place wasn't as bad as he'd drawn it.

Still, Ron's friend had pretty much said the same thing. If it was that horrid, it might explain the nightmares that had haunted her for twenty years. An old church. Dark, steep steps. A baby crying. Orphanages surely had crying babies.

Her mood was far too somber now. She was sorry she'd read the article. She walked to the kitchen, dumped what was left of her salad down the disposal and took the winding stairs to the second floor, where Frederick Lee ruled over a much more hospitable past.

She opened the closet and pulled out the box in which she'd first found the teal satin dress. The garment was now hanging in her closet, ready to be worn to this year's Heritage Ball, which would be held on the final night of the spring pilgrimage.

But there were surely other Billingham treasures waiting to be discovered and break her dismal mood, especially on a night when she should be celebrating.

She'd kept her job. Trudy was recovering and had given Sam vital information that would soon lead to the arrest of the Prentice Park Killer. And she'd had one wonderful night of lovemaking. No matter what happened between Sam and her, she'd always have that.

This time she chose another box. It was stuffed into the back of the closet and harder to get to. She opened it and pulled out a scrapbook. The pages were yellowed, but it was filled with old newspaper clippings. And a wedding picture. The bride was beautiful, dressed in a simple but exquisite white gown set with tiny pearls.

Margie Billingham, wed to the Reverend Thomas Cleary, February 18, 1904. And she'd been wed right here in this house. Caroline could picture her walking down the winding staircase with all her family and friends watching as she married the man of her dreams.

"You sired a great family, Frederick Lee." She sat on the sofa and looked through the scrapbook, careful not to damage the frayed pages. Packed beneath the scrapbook was a stack of letters, tied with twine. All addressed to Margie Billingham.

Caroline slid the first one from the tattered envelope. It was a love letter from Thomas. Captivated with the sweetness of his words and the depth of his feeling, she read every one.

But the box had more. There was something wrapped in layers of tissue. Caroline pushed the paper aside, then oohed and ahhed as she pulled out the wedding dress from the old black-and-white photo. It was yellowed, but so gorgeous it took her breath away.

She held it up to her shoulders, but knew that would never be enough. She shed her clothes in record time and pulled the dress over her head. It was tight across her bosom, a little loose around the waist, but she felt as if she'd stepped back in time.

She stood in front of the mirror. As always the wavy glass distorted her image, made her look surreal, almost a ghost bride.

She twirled. Ghostly or not, the dress swishing around her ankles felt divine. Not wanting to take it off, she swept down the staircase in it. The marvelous find called for a glass of wine. She used one of two antique crystal flutes she'd found at a flea market the month before and took it back to her desk.

She logged back onto the Internet and pulled up her e-mail. Now there were twenty-eight messages. The last one was from someone she'd never heard of, but the subject line got her attention.

To my sweet Daphne.

The words filled her with dread. It might just be someone who'd read the tabloid about her changing her name and wanted to slam her. She should just delete it, but she didn't dare. It could be from the killer. He had to be stopped. One way or the other, he had to be stopped. So she moved on and read his message.

Hello, Daphne

I'm thinking of you, though I'm not happy you spent last night with Sam Turner. I had hoped you were saving yourself for me. But then, you don't really know me yet. You will soon. And you'll discover how very much we have in common. Much more than you have with Sam. He hasn't suffered as we have. But he will. Trust me, he will.

Take care, Daphne. Our destiny is upon us.

Sick! The guy was totally and completely depraved. Why did he keep coming at her like this? What made him think she was like him in any way?

She wanted to scream or throw something or bang her head against a wall. But she couldn't even delete his disgusting message. Sam would want to see it.

Catch him quickly, Sam. Get him off the streets before he slices up someone else. But the truth was they didn't know for sure if the guy contacting her was the man who'd murdered Sally and Ruby. He never said anything that unmistakably tied him to the crimes. He could just be a crazy who got his rocks off tormenting her.

Caroline dialed Sam's number. She got a busy signal. She pushed back from the computer, wanting to get as far away from the message as she could. She went back to the front of the house, still wearing the exquisite wedding dress, but it had lost its magic.

She stopped off in the kitchen to refill her wine-glass, then hurried past the door to the basement the way she always did. But this time there was more than the chilly blast of cold air. There was the sound of crying.

She stood very still, her body frozen to the spot, though her heart was pounding against the wall of her chest. She was losing it. Letting a deranged killer drive her absolutely mad.

But she heard the sound again. A baby's cry. Soft, but unmistakable. It was the cry from the night-mare…but nightmares weren't real. Nightmares couldn't hurt you, not unless you let them steal your sanity.

And she wouldn't let them. She wrapped her hand around the doorknob and eased the door open. She tried to flick on the light, but either the bulb was missing from the fixture or it had burned out. But there was enough light from the hallway that she could see down the steep, narrow steps to the dark-ness below.

She didn't see a baby, but something moved in the shadows and she heard the cry again. The wave of fear that hit her was deep and strong, pulling her under and back into the past. Back to the dark, damp hell where ghost babies cried in the wall.

"Let's all three hold hands. If we stay together, they won't hurt us. Just hold on tight and be very, very quiet."

Caroline held on. As tightly as she could. But the baby just kept crying. And whatever it was that moved in the shadows inched closer.

Chapter Twelve

Sam slowed as he passed Caroline's house. It was late, but her lights were still on. He wondered what she'd say if he knocked on her door this time of the night. For that matter, what *would* he say?

The truth sounded corny for a man his age. *I've been thinking about you all day—in and around attempts to locate the murderous Billy Smith, instead of the thousand law-abiding ones. I like sleeping on your floor.* Or the ever popular, *I'm horny as hell and I'd like to make love to you again.*

Actually, he just wanted to be with her. If she didn't want to be with him tonight, she could always kick him out. He parked the car and hurried up the walk.

He rang the doorbell and waited. Then he rang it again. Still no response, but there were lights on all over the house. She had to be in there.

This time he pounded on the door. "Caroline!"

His cop instincts kicked in with a rush of adrenaline. He had her key somewhere. He rummaged through his pockets until he found it. He called her name again as he shoved open the door.

The drawing room was empty, but the door to the basement was open. He ran to it, then stopped. She was sprawled across the steps, a white dress spread all around her, her head at an awkward angle against one of the balusters.

He ran down the steps and gathered her in his arms. She looked up at him, her eyes wide.

"Sam?"

"It's me. I'm here, baby."

"How did you get here?"

"I just stopped by. I had your key so I came in." There was no blood and she was talking, though she seemed confused, almost as if she'd been in some kind of hypnotic trance. "What happened here, Caroline? Did you fall?"

"I think I passed out, or maybe I slipped on the steps. I don't remember."

"Why were you down here in the dark?"

"I heard a noise. It sounded like a baby crying, like in my nightmares. But I knew it couldn't be real."

"So you came down here in the dark to prove that?"

"The light's burned out."

"Have you ever blacked out like this before?"

"No. But I think it's just dealing with all the madness. It all got to me at once and I started having strange thoughts, as if I were remembering something from long ago. I think it's memories from back when I was at Meyers Bickham."

"More fallout from that stupid tabloid article."

"I guess. They mentioned the place and then someone at work brought it up again today."

The children's home from hell. Sam had heard the horror stories long before he met Caroline, but hadn't really believed them then.

He swooped her up in his arms and started up the steps. Suddenly, he felt her stiffen at a sound—but he'd heard it, too, and he'd never been to Meyers Bickham. He sat her down at the top of the stairs. His right hand flew to the gun in his shoulder holster, but when the culprit sprang out of the darkness, he didn't shoot.

"A cat," Caroline said. "I was frightened out of my skull by a cat."

"Do you have some milk?" Sam asked. "If you do, we can probably coax it up here. And I need a flashlight so I can figure out how it got into your basement."

"The flashlight's by my bed, third door down the hall. You get that. I'll get the milk."

Sam watched her hurry toward the kitchen, dressed in the long white gown, her short hair bouncing about her head. She looked like a vision. Or a bride. Desire slammed into him with the force of a runaway train. He had it bad.

CAROLINE STROKED the cat while Sam searched the basement. She'd slipped out of the wedding dress and into a soft silk robe. No reason to risk getting milk or cat hairs on the antique gown.

The cat was scrunched up in her lap and purring contentedly. "You precious little thing, how in the world did you get in my basement? That's okay— you were probably as frightened as I was, though you didn't pass out. You handle fear well. Good kitty."

"Looks like you made friends fast," Sam said, returning to the kitchen, flashlight still in hand.

"Animals like me."

"And that empty saucer on the floor wouldn't have a thing to do with that, I guess."

"She'd have liked me, anyway. She just likes me better now."

"It's that slow hand with the stroking."

She had the feeling he wasn't only referring to her stroking the cat's back. A flush crept to her cheeks, but it felt good. Being with Sam felt good. "Did you find out how she got in?"

"Yep. You have a broken window."

Her heart jumped to her throat as the terror set in again. "The killer?"

"It could have been neighborhood kids."

"I've never had problems with them before."

"Could have been a common thief. There's a lot of stuff down there."

"You don't believe that, Sam, and neither do I."

"Well, if it was Billy Smith, you won't have to worry much longer. He'll be in custody soon. And I'll fix that window first thing tomorrow and have metal grates installed over the glass."

"Dare I ask how the search for Billy Smith is going?"

"There are a lot of Billy Smiths in the state of Georgia. A slew of them just in this county. And then there are all the Billy or William Smiths in neighboring states and the strong likelihood that Billy Smith is an alias."

"So what do you do? Wade through them all, hoping to find something that indicates he might be the one?''

''I have an artist flying in from San Antonio in the morning, the best in the business.''

''I suppose an accurate picture would make a world of difference.''

''Especially if this guy has a record, and I'm almost certain that he will.''

''Did you check to see if anyone in Georgia by the name of Billy Smith had a record?''

''I have a team working on that now. Meanwhile, there's no proof that Billy Smith is the one who murdered the two victims.''

''Well, I'm convinced it's Billy and I'm counting on your artist delivering such a great likeness that he's arrested within the hour of circulating the sketch.''

''I hope you're right. I'd appreciate it if you could be at the hospital tomorrow morning when the artist is there. Trudy seems a lot more relaxed when you're around.''

''She seems to have bonded with me. I'm not sure why.''

''You're easy to bond with.''

He meant it as a compliment, but it hit the wrong chord. ''Apparently too easy. I heard from him again tonight, Sam.''

He crossed the room and placed his hands on her shoulders. ''Did you record the voice?''

''It wasn't a phone call this time. It was an e-mail. But in a way, that's good, isn't it? Can you check the address he sent it from and find out where he is?''

"On the unlikely chance that he used his own e-mail account."

"But even if used a friend's, couldn't you find and question that person?"

"If the guy's as smart as past experience indicates, he probably used a computer at a public library or some Internet café. Actually it's pretty easy to just walk into a large office building these days, step into an empty office and log on to the Internet."

"Wouldn't he need a password?"

"Computers in a library or Internet café are already online. So are the computers in half the offices in town. People are supposed to sign off public computers, but they don't always. So the next person goes up and there's the previous user's ID. We had a case last month of a stolen identity, and that's how the guy got the information."

"Modern crime."

"And technologically adept criminals. So let's see this e-mail."

She sighed. The cat jumped from her lap. "I'd scatter, too, if I were you," she said.

Sam followed her back to her office and she pulled up the message. He read it, then slammed his right fist into his left hand.

"Do you think it's from Billy?" Caroline asked.

"He may not be Billy, but he's obsessed with you and obviously watching everything you do. He knows I spent the night here last night. He probably knows I'm here now."

She touched Sam's arm. The muscles were taut. He was as disturbed by this latest contact as she was.

"Is my broken basement window large enough for a man to squeeze though?"

"If he's skinny."

"Or average size?"

"I'll see that those grates are installed tomorrow. Strong ones that'll take a blowtorch to get through."

"And tonight?"

He put a thumb under her chin and tilted it so that she met his gaze. She saw concern there, a touch of fury, but also desire. The same desire she felt every time he was near.

"If you sleep with a cop," he said, "you'll always be safe."

"Do you have any particular cop in mind?"

His answer was a kiss. She melted against him, loving the feel of his strong arms around her and his solid chest to lean on.

Always safe when you sleep with a cop.

Unless he broke her heart.

SAM WAS WITH HER again. Had his stinking cop hands all over her. So disgusting, it made him sick to think about it. They were pushing him too far. Sam Turner always pushed too far. But he wouldn't get away with it.

Caroline was meant to be his. He'd paid the price. He had a right to her. They were bonded in a way she and Sam could never bond. When she learned the truth of who he was, she'd know that, too. There would be one more death. And then Caroline would be his forever.

He stared at the rambling old house as the last light went out, and he hated Sam Turner clear down to his soul.

SAM AWOKE with his arm around Caroline and her naked body pressed against his. He eased his arm from under her and slid off the bed, being careful not to wake her. For the second night in a row, they'd made love. For the second night in a row, it had been exciting and passionate and right.

He hadn't expected it to happen this way, would never have believed he could have slipped into intimacy so easily. But then, that was how it had happened with Peg, too. He'd been knee-deep in a murder case, so involved that he hadn't seen the relationship coming. Maybe that was what it took to get him past the bad notions about relationships he'd learned at his mother's knee—and on the receiving end of his stepfather's belt.

Now here he was, so involved in a case that he hardly even had time to breathe regularly and he was sleeping with a reporter. In her bed. In her arms.

He walked through the house, stopping to check the lock on the basement door. He didn't know how the window had gotten broken, but it had happened recently. Otherwise the basement would been have cluttered with leaves and debris.

Besides, he knew that the cop patrolling the area was keeping a close watch on the house, even walking around it and making a visual inspection at least a couple of times a day, and he hadn't reported a broken window.

And that left the very real possibility that the man who was stalking Caroline had made an effort to move beyond notes and phone calls. If he'd been successful in his break-in attempt, it could have been him waiting when Caroline opened the door to the basement, instead of a cat.

The image of that ripped along Sam's nerves and burned like pure acid in his stomach. There had to be answers out there somewhere. He just had to find them. Right now his best chance was riding on Josephine. In the meantime, he had to keep Caroline safe.

And he had to stay focused. It was the little things that usually broke a case like this.

He went over tonight's e-mail message again in his mind. The man was obsessed with Caroline. He hated that Sam had stayed over, and he'd mentioned Sam by name. Could this possibly be someone he knew? Someone who'd hated him even before the murders had started? Someone he'd arrested in the past—someone like R.J.?

Not likely, but he never ruled out any possibilities. He drank a glass of water, then rummaged in the refrigerator and took out a chunk of cheddar cheese. The knives were stored in a wooden block on the counter. He reached for the smallest one, but stopped at the sound of footfalls in the hall.

He recognized the soft tread, and his heart knocked around in his chest. "I thought you were sound asleep," he said when Caroline reached the door.

"I was, but I woke up and missed you."

His focus dissolved. Caroline had pulled on the yellow silk robe she'd worn earlier tonight, but it was half-open, revealing a glimpse of her from her neck all the way to her toes. Soft breasts. Smooth skin fading to a triangle of dark curly hair. The cheese slipped from his hands.

"If you're hungry, I can fix you something."

He couldn't take his eyes off her, could barely talk, and when he did his voice was gravelly and steeped in desire. "I'm hungry, but what I want is already fixed."

"Then come to bed, Sam. Come back and we'll feast."

But his blood was rushing, his whole body shaking with a raw hunger that didn't even seem to belong to him. He pulled her into his arms, crushing her mouth with his as he pushed the robe from her shoulders.

They made love standing up, her back against the wall, him pushing into her. It was hot and fevered, like a rafting trip over the falls, wet and primal, so wild he thought his heart might bolt right out of his chest.

It ended as fast as it had begun, with both of them still holding on to each other and their breaths coming in choppy gasps.

Caroline burrowed her face in his chest. "Wow! I didn't know you had that in you, Detective."

"Neither did I, Reporter Lady. Neither did I."

SAM KNEW SOMETHING was wrong when he awoke in the gray hour just before dawn and saw Caroline curled up in the chair by the window. He stretched, then got up and joined her, resting his backside against the windowsill.

"It's early," he said.

"I know," she replied, "but I couldn't sleep and I didn't want to wake you with my tossing."

"I know how hard this must be on you."

"Do you, Sam?"

"I think so. I'm not a woman, and so I don't know exactly what it's like to be stalked by a madman, but I know it must be frightening."

"I wasn't thinking about the murders this morning."

"If it's your past, you have to let all that go. You can't change that your mother was irresponsible. It's she who was the real loser."

"Did you forget your past, Sam?"

"I try not to think about how I was raised."

"But what about Peg? Do you still think about her, Sam?"

And here it was, all out in the open. Sam had known this moment would come eventually, but he wasn't ready for it. Yet he owed Caroline an honest answer.

Chapter Thirteen

Sam stared out the window, letting his thoughts slide back to the night he'd first met Peg. She'd been young, vulnerable, frightened. He exhaled slowly, catching his breath and searching his mind for the right words. "I think about her."

"Are you still in love with her?"

He had to tread carefully here. He wouldn't lie to Caroline, but he didn't want to lie to himself, either. "How much do you know about her?" he asked, instead.

"Just what Matt told me. That she's been dead for seven years. But her picture is still on display in your den and it's the only photograph in your house. Was she your wife?"

"No. We lived together for a little less than a year, but we never married. She didn't want to marry, said it would ruin the relationship. She had lots of crazy ideas like that."

"But you loved her with all her crazy ideas."

"I did. She was the best thing that ever happened to me."

"How did you meet her?"

"I was on a case, working long hours, never sleeping, living on aspirin and coffee. One night when I was tracking down a suspect in a liquor-store robbery, she stepped out of the shadows and asked me to arrest her for prostitution."

"Was she a prostitute?"

"She was. Nineteen years old and working the streets, but she looked more like fifteen. She had long blond hair and incredibly blue eyes, and when she looked at me… Anyway, I didn't have the heart to arrest her, but I knew she was afraid of something, so I took her home with me."

"Just like that?"

"Just like that. I was only thirty, but I felt eons older than her. She was so vulnerable and haunted. She never told me what she was afraid of, just stayed there in my house and loved me. No one ever had until she did."

"What happened? How did she die?"

"She was murdered in our apartment. I knew she was afraid again, but I thought it was for me. I ignored the signs. I let it happen. I was so caught up in apprehending a cop killer that I let her get killed."

"Did you find the man who killed her?"

"No. But I tried. I went crazy trying. And drinking myself into a stupor night after night when I couldn't crack the case. The one person in all my life who'd loved me and counted on me, and I let her down. After two years of screwing up my life, the chief told me to get my act together and stop spending all my time on a cold case or be fired."

"What did you do?"

"I quit, moved back to Georgia. Lived in Atlanta

for a while, then took this job in Prentice. I've been here four years. And now you know it all.''

"And you're still blaming yourself for Peg's death?"

"I guess." He ran his fingers through his hair, pushing it back from his face. "No, I don't guess. I know. I still blame myself. If there had been closure, if her killer had been caught, it might be different, but the guy is still walking the streets a free man."

"What about your cop killer?"

"Him I got, but now he's back on the streets, too. He was my stepbrother, R. J. Blocker. Now there's a worthless piece of trash."

"End of story," Caroline said.

Only it wasn't. Not yet. He knelt by the chair and took Caroline's hands in his. "You asked me if I was still in love with Peg."

"You answered, Sam. You may not have meant to, but you did. I just have to know one other thing."

"Anything."

"Do I remind you of her? Is that what attracted you to me?"

"A little at first, but that's not why I'm here now."

"It's because I'm afraid, isn't it? You see the same fear in me that you saw in her, and you think you have to protect me. You think I need you, that I'm weak."

"You, weak?" He tilted her head and kept his thumb under her chin so that she had to meet his gaze. "You're not weak, Caroline. You're a survivor. A trash can with maggots, Meyers Bickham, being stalked by a vicious murderer—nothing destroys you.

You're stronger than Peg ever was, stronger than I am.''

He pulled her into his arms. She tried to push him away, but he wouldn't let her. From the moment he'd started talking, things had become clearer in his mind. He still didn't understand everything about his feelings and probably never would, but he was dead certain of one thing. He did not want to lose Caroline.

''I'm not in love with Peg, but I am in love with you. And I don't think my heart could survive losing you.''

''Oh, Sam. Are you sure? Are you very, very sure, because I don't want to love you only to lose you to a memory.''

A tear rolled down her cheek. He kissed it away. ''I'm very, very sure. And not because you're weak, or strong, or that you remind me of anyone else. I just love you because you're you.''

''And I love you, Sam. With all my heart. I never thought love could come in two short weeks.''

''It didn't. It came in a lifetime of working our way toward this moment and each other.''

He picked her up and carried her back to bed. He just wanted to hold her and wait for the dawn.

JOSEPHINE STERLING was not at all the way Caroline had imagined. She'd pictured her thin and willowy, with long, nimble fingers to wield her pencil. Instead, she was big-boned and her fingers were short and chunky. But she had long, flaming red hair that seemed to go in a dozen directions at once, and a great smile. She might have been as old as fifty or as young as thirty. There was no way to tell.

Sam made the introductions and Josephine took over from there. There was no real reason for Caroline to be there, since Josephine had a way about her that put everyone at ease.

Everyone, that is, except Trudy's mother. Mrs. Mitchell stayed this time, but moved to the other side of the room. Josephine pulled a chair up to the bed, commenting on the number of signatures on Trudy's cast while she readied her sketch pad.

"All the nurses signed it. And my guards."

"I saw today's guard when I came in. Kinda cute. I'm thinking I should see if he'll model for a couple of sketches."

"That's Kirk. He's my favorite. And he's not married."

"All right. Nothing better than having a cute cop around to keep you company. I've had the same one around for almost twenty-five years now. I've about decided he's a keeper."

"So are you married?" Trudy asked.

"Very married." Josephine twirled the simple gold band on her ring finger. "And we have three children, all girls. Very smart kids. None of them wants to be a cop or artist."

Caroline was impressed. If Josephine was as good at sketching as she was at getting the witness to relax, this could be a very informative session.

"I won't have guards after today." Trudy informed Josephine. "I'm going home this afternoon."

That was news to Caroline. From the look on Sam's face, it was news to him, too.

Trudy and Josephine chatted for a few more minutes, mostly about how Josephine got into this line of work. Then Josephine eased Trudy into the description. "So tell me what you remember about this man I'm going to be drawing."

"What do you want to know first?"

"Start anywhere. I'll follow along and if I get lost, I'll stop and ask directions. I can do that since I'm a woman."

Trudy smiled, but she was tightening up again. She closed her eyes for a second, then stared at her hands. "Billy's got a regular face. He's just average, you know, but kind of cute. You wouldn't think a guy like that could be cute, but he is."

"Evil often comes gift-wrapped in pretty packages. Tell me about his hair."

"It's blond. He wears it short." Trudy used her hand to indicate a length above the collar. "But it's longer in front. Kinda falls in his face sometimes."

"So he doesn't keep it sprayed in place?"

"No. His hair always looks a little mussed, but not the rest of him. He's preppie. Wears name-brand stuff. Expensive tennis shoes. That kind of dresser."

"I see. What about his eyes?"

"They're pale blue. They're his most striking feature."

That was new. Caroline didn't remember Trudy having mentioned it before.

"His nose is just average. So is his mouth. No, that's not exactly true. His mouth kind of turns up more in one corner than it does the other."

"Like this?" Josephine held up the drawing for Trudy to examine.

"Yes, except it's the right side that turns up."

Josephine altered the sketch. "Look at the eyes. Is this how Billy's look?"

Trudy twirled a finger in her hair. "Not exactly. Maybe they're not quite so round."

Josephine altered the sketch again. "Is this better?"

"It's closer, but still not right. It may be the brows that are wrong."

"Are Billy's thinner than I drew them?"

"They don't come that close together in the middle."

Caroline moved back to stand beside Mrs. Mitchell. From the look on her face and the way she was chewing on her bottom lip, she needed more reassurance than Trudy did. Neither of them could see the sketch from this angle, but Caroline could tell from the questions and responses that they were getting closer to having it right.

It was a fascinating process, a kind of tweaking and fine-tuning at each point until it matched what the witness was describing. Josephine would concentrate on one part of the face for a while, then move to another feature, back and forth, like working a jigsaw puzzle where you constructed the pieces as you went.

It was about forty minutes into the session before Trudy started nodding a lot. "That's close, Josephine. Real close. There's still something that's not quite right, but I can't put my finger on it."

Sam moved so that he could get a better look at the sketch. He frowned. Apparently the sketch didn't fit anyone he'd questioned in either of the murders.

When he moved back, Caroline stepped over for her first look since real progress had been made.

Oh, this hurt. This really, really hurt.

"Try to think, Trudy, what should I change?"

"It's his nose," Caroline said, forcing the words from her dry throat. "The nose is wrong. It's narrower and shorter."

She shuddered and Sam was by her side in an instant. He put an arm around her shoulders. "You know this man?"

She nodded and fought her panic as Josephine made the changes.

"That's him, isn't it, Trudy?" Caroline asked. But she didn't need to wait for a verbal response. It was written all over Trudy's face.

"I know him," Caroline said, "but not as Billy. I know him as Jack Smith. He's engaged to my best friend, Becky."

BINGO! THIS WAS a hundred times better than Sam had hoped. Not only did he have a suspect, he had people who knew the guy, and probably where he lived. Sure, he was sorry for Caroline's friend, but better Becky found out now than after the wedding, or after the family was called to identify her body in the local morgue.

"I have to call Becky and warn her," Caroline said as Sam herded her to his car.

"No phone calls."

"Becky's not a criminal, Sam. She's not in this with Jack."

"She may not be a criminal, but she's a woman in love."

"What's that supposed to mean?"

"We call it the stand-by-your-man syndrome. Some women think they have to remain loyal no matter what. It happens with men, too, just not as often."

"Becky wouldn't do that, not once she knows the truth."

"No phone calls," he repeated. He opened the passenger door for her, then hightailed it around the car and climbed behind the wheel. "Do you know how to get in touch with Billy, or Jack, or whoever he turns out to be?"

"No, but I'm sure Becky does."

"Then let's pay her a visit. Where do we find her?"

"She owns Bon Appetit, and she's usually there this time of the morning. It's a gourmet deli on Front Street."

"I know it. Matt dragged me in there once. He was probably hitting on your friend."

"Too bad she didn't fall for *him*."

"She may have. But this was months ago and a week's a long-term affair to Matt."

"Great partner you have."

"He's a good cop." Sam was making conversation, but his mind was already working out details for what he hoped was going to be a swift arrest. He'd get Matt to do the paperwork for an arrest warrant. And he'd check with Atlanta, see if Jack Smith had a record. This time he'd have a likeness to send them. If the guy was trouble, they'd know it.

He was probably breaking some kind of rule taking Caroline with him, her being a reporter and all, but he might need her help in dealing with her friend Becky. And this way, he didn't have to worry about Jack finding Caroline before they found him.

Obsessed with Caroline. Engaged to her best friend. It didn't compute. But then, they still had no proof that Jack was the killer they were looking for, much less that he was the one tormenting Caroline. Hopefully, the chips were about to start falling into place.

Damn traffic was too slow for a town this size. That was what happened when people obeyed the speed limit. He reached under his seat, pulled out his portable light and siren, flicked it on and stuck in on the dash. "When did you meet Jack?"

"The first time was at Becky's birthday party. The same night Sally Martin was murdered."

"Whoa. He was at a party the night of the first murder?"

"Yes, but he left early."

"How early?"

"A good half hour before I got the call from John ordering me to Freedom Park."

"A half hour to find a victim, kill her and call the local TV channel and newspaper. That's cutting it close."

"But it had to be him, Sam. Why else would he have warned Trudy not to tell us that he'd been hanging around the restaurant and necking in the parking lot with Sally?"

"But he wasn't in the restaurant the day you stopped by. So the only way he could have known she'd talked to you would be if someone told him."

"He *was* there. I didn't see him, but I'm sure of it. He's everywhere. I don't how he does it, but he seems to know everything I do and everywhere I go."

Sam swerved into a loading zone near the restaurant. "I think this may go better if you do the talking. Don't mention I'm a cop or that this has anything to do with the murders until we talk to Becky in private."

Bon Appetit was already full even though it was just after 10 a.m. Coffeehouses were finally in vogue in Prentice.

Caroline went to the counter by the cash register. "Is Becky in? I need to talk to her."

"No, she took the day off. I guess you heard her big news."

"The news that she's engaged?"

"What else?"

"Did Becky say where she'd be today?"

"No, but I got the impression she was going somewhere with Jack."

"But she didn't say where?"

"No. Is something wrong? You look really upset."

"I need to get in touch with her right away. Do you know how to reach Jack?"

"Don't have a clue. You might try Becky's parents. Or you can try calling her at home. She may not have left yet."

"Thanks, and if you talk to her, tell her to call me at once. Tell her it's very important."

"Gotcha."

CAROLINE WAS SHAKING when she got back in the car. Sam reached across the seat, took her hand and squeezed it.

"Don't jump to conclusions, Caroline. There's no reason to think Becky's in danger."

"She's with a heartless, brutal killer."

"That's possible, but she's apparently been with him often. They're engaged."

"More than that, Sam. She told me yesterday they're planning to elope."

He groaned. "Then they could be anywhere. Tell me about her parents."

"Her dad is Dr. Scott Simpson. He's a pediatrician with an office next door to Prentice Hospital. Her mother doesn't work. They live near the country club."

"Try to reach Becky at home. If she's there, tell her you need to talk to her and ask her to stay home until you get there. Don't tell her the reason for the visit."

"She's got to know sometime, Sam."

"Jack could be there. If you alert him something's wrong, he'll bolt."

"Or hurt Becky. Oh, Sam...let's just drive by there. It's not far."

"Okay. In the meantime, go ahead and call her mother. If she doesn't know how to get in touch with Becky, see if she knows how to reach Jack. A phone number. His parents' name. Where they live. Anything. And I know you're upset, but try to stay calm."

She was about as calm as the ocean in the middle of a hurricane. Still, she managed to carry on what she hoped was a halfway sane conversation with Mrs. Simpson.

"What did you find out?" Sam asked the second she broke the connection.

"Becky's not at home. She called her mother about an hour ago to say she was going off for a few days with Jack."

Sam slammed a fist against the steering wheel. "Did she give you any information about Jack?"

"He lives with his parents just south of Gadsden, Alabama, which is about a two-hour drive from Prentice. She doesn't have an address but his dad owns a car dealership in Gadsden."

"That should do it. I have to stop off at the station to take care of some paperwork and talk to the Gadsden police. After that, I'll drop you off at the newspaper, but I don't want you to leave the office today. I'll have one of the guys pick you up after work, take you home and stay there with you until I get back."

"No."

"No to which part of that?"

"No to all of it. I'm going with you."

"This is police business."

"And it's mine. Do you have any idea what it's like to know someone you care about is in danger?"

"I do." His tone was solemn as if her words had sucked the fight right out of him. He reached over and squeezed her hand. "You can go, but I have to handle this. If Jack's guilty, I'm not going to have him walk on a technicality."

"Thanks, Sam."

She wanted to be there on the scene while this

played out, but even getting her way with that didn't ease the apprehension that had seized her heart.

ALBERT JACKSON SMITH was well-known by the Gadsden Police Department and had been since he was fifteen years old. He was twenty-eight now. As a juvenile he'd been arrested for burglarizing a house and stealing guns and ammunition, hauled in on charges of sexual battery against a fourteen-year-old girl and accused of poisoning his neighbor's dog.

None of the charges had stuck and he'd never spent more than a couple of days in a juvenile facility. His dad had influence and big bucks.

As an adult he'd been arrested several times for drug possession, three times for disorderly conduct and once for simple battery. None of those charges had stuck, either. According to the detective Sam had talked to, Jack was savvy, a pathological liar, and for some reason, witnesses against him always dropped charges before a case went to trial. Sam had a good idea why.

But this time a witness had talked. If nothing else, they could arrest him for attempted rape and hold him while they investigated the two murders. There was already an APB out on him and the sketch had been sent to every police department in Georgia, Alabama and the surrounding states.

He had no idea why Jack had given a false name to Trudy and Sally and his real name to Becky, but suspected it had to do with Becky's socioeconomic standing. He might have had plans to worm his way into her life permanently from the very beginning.

Sam pulled up in front of the car dealership owned

by Jack's father. It was impressive, a big lot with a huge supply of new vehicles and quite a few used but late-model cars lined up and glittering in the afternoon sun. The showroom, all gleaming steel and plate glass, was the latest in sleek, modern architecture. Unless there were some serious management problems, the Smiths did not want for cash.

Sam parked in the customer area. "That's our guy in the green car," Sam said. "Detective Williams from the Gadsden Police Department. Right on time."

"Will he do the talking," Caroline asked, "or will you?"

"I'm pitching the game. He's just here to make it all legal, since this is out of my jurisdiction."

"Will you tell Mr. Smith that his son is wanted for murder?"

"All depends on how I read him. Half of detective work is gut instinct. The other half is luck. We need both today."

He reached across the seat and touched Caroline's shoulder, letting his fingers tangle for a second in the soft locks of her hair. He almost felt guilty for getting the kind of adrenaline rush he always got when he was closing in on a suspect, especially when he knew how tough this was on her. But she was hanging in there. Soft as a kitten. Tough as a Doberman.

JACK DID NOT GET his looks from this father, Caroline decided as the short, balding man with the extra-large spare tire protruding over his belt led them into a luxurious office. His face was the color of Georgia clay, but his eyes were the same striking pale blue as his son's.

He was smiling broadly when he closed the door to his office, but his expression became agitated as soon as Sam introduced himself and the other detective as police officers.

"We're trying to locate your son, Jack. Do you know where we can find him?"

"What did he do?"

"Maybe nothing, but we'd like to ask him a few questions."

"Do you have a warrant?"

"As a matter of fact I do. So do you know how we can reach him?"

"He's twenty-eight years old. I don't follow him around."

"I was under the impression that he works here."

"He's off this week, on vacation somewhere."

"And you don't have any idea how to reach him?"

"I don't have a clue."

"Does he have a cell phone?"

"When he's working, he uses one of the company ones, but he doesn't take it with him when he's off. Says he likes to get away from everything. You know how kids his age are."

"Twenty-eight's not exactly a kid, Mr. Smith."

"You're right, and whatever he's done now, I'm not responsible."

"You're only responsible if you cover up for him."

"What is it you're accusing him of?"

"We just want to talk to him."

The Gadsden cop pulled a business card from his shirt pocket. "When you hear from him, have him call me. My number's on the card." When the guy didn't reach to take it, Williams dropped it on top of his desk. "He can call either number. Any time, day or night."

The man glared at him, then looked at Caroline. His gaze seemed to bore right through her, and she felt as if she'd been touched by something dirty, sordid. Jack didn't get his looks from his father, but she'd bet he'd gotten his sick sexual ways from him. Maybe even his appetite for murder.

"Just have Jack call, Mr. Smith," Sam said, his tone almost threatening. "Unless we find him first."

ALBERT JACKSON SENIOR watched the two arrogant detectives and the woman drive out of the parking lot. They thought they were so smart. But they hadn't fooled him for a second. He recognized Sam Turner from TV and newspaper coverage of the Prentice murders.

Jack was in big trouble this time. That part was no surprise. He just kept pushing the envelope further and further. That was why he'd been ordered out of the house and cut off from his funds.

But murder? Albert never thought his son would go that far. He didn't want to believe it now.

And he wouldn't. Not until he knew for sure. But this time he was scared. He locked the door. He needed privacy for the phone call he was about to make. He went back, lifted the receiver and dialed his son's cell-phone number.

No matter what he'd done, Jack was still his son. He had to be warned.

IT WAS FIVE-THIRTY by the time Caroline got back to the newspaper office. Most of the reporters and clerical staff had gone for the day, but a few remained. And John and the printing crew were in the back setting up for the next morning's edition.

The APB was still out for Jack, along with Josephine's sketch and a picture of Becky that Caroline had provided, but there'd been no reports of anyone seeing them. Sam was at the police station and would be for several more hours.

He'd suggested she go home and rest—with a cop along as bodyguard just in case Jack was crazy enough to come after her. But she was too keyed up to rest. Better to be at work and staying busy.

She turned on her computer monitor. The story couldn't break yet, but she wanted to write something on composite sketching while it was still fresh in her mind. It was only when she started to type that her mind switched gears and she wrote what flowed into it.

Albert Jackson Smith had everything. A family. Money. Nice clothes. Good looks. But somewhere along the way his mind became a cesspool, festering and suppurating until it was so diseased he no longer separated right from wrong. And in that sick and depraved state, he took the lives of two young women—

The ring of her cell phone startled her and sent her heart rate spiraling. She checked the digital read-out. The number was Becky's. Her heart leaped to her throat as she hit the talk button and took the call.

"Becky. Where are you?"

"She's with me, and if you ever want to see her alive again, you better listen and listen good."

Chapter Fourteen

"Jack. Where are you? Where's Becky?"

"I said for you to listen, not ask questions."

"The police know all about you. You can't get away with this. You have to give yourself up."

"All the police know is what that lying bitch who works at the Catfish Shack told them."

"Then don't hurt Becky. Just come back to town and tell the police the truth."

"Well, that would be a lot easier, wouldn't it, if you and your detective friend weren't trying to pin those two murders on me."

"You told Trudy your name was Billy and you threatened her."

"Yeah, I did that. And I ran her into the ditch 'cause she has a big mouth and I knew sooner or later she was going to talk. But I didn't kill anybody and I'm not taking the rap."

She didn't believe him, but if she told him that, it would only put Becky in more danger. She had to reason with him if there was any reasoning with a madman. "No one's trying to pin anything on you,

Jack, but the police need to hear your side of the story.''

"Oh, yeah. That's the police, all right. They're always just looking for the truth and trying to help out guys like me.''

"They are if you're innocent.''

"Nobody's innocent, Caroline. Certainly not the stinking cops.''

"Where's Becky?''

"She's with me.''

"Let me talk to her.''

"That's why I called, sweetheart, for you to do that. You started this when you went to see my dad.''

"No one mentioned the murders to your father, I swear.''

"He's not stupid. When the detective heading up the Prentice Park Killer investigation comes calling on him in the middle of the day, he doesn't think it's because I stole money from a drink machine.''

"What do you want me to tell Becky?''

"That you know the cops are planning to pin the murders on me just because the flake at the Catfish Shack said I dated Sally Martin a few times. Tell Becky to run with me. And you better do a damn good job of convincing her. If you fail, I'll kill her. But I won't waste my time finding a park or cutting her throat. I'll shoot her so full of holes she'll look like Swiss cheese.''

"*You* go on the run, Jack. Just don't take Becky with you. You'll have a better chance of getting away by yourself.''

"But I'd be a lot poorer.''

"So this was never about love or your actually wanting to marry her. It's about her money."

"Aw, Caroline, you are indeed a smart woman. Stay that way. You convince her to go with me willingly, and she lives. If she causes trouble, I kill her. Easy choice, sweetheart. So what'll it be?"

It was no choice at all. She had to buy time. "Put her on the phone, Jack."

"Okay. Hold on, and I'll get her."

"Get her from where?"

"Don't worry. She's just in the shower—this time."

There had to be a way to handle this, a way to let Becky know what was going on and still keep her safe. But all Caroline could think of was Sally and Ruby. Dead.

"Hi, Caroline."

Caroline exhaled slowly, fighting panic, trying to think what to say. "Are you okay?"

"No. I'm so upset. I just want to go home, but Jack's begging me to go with him."

"Go where?"

"I don't know. On a plane somewhere out of the country. His dad said a couple of cops came to see him today. He thinks Jack's going to be arrested for murdering those two women in Prentice. He didn't do it. I know he didn't, but he doesn't think the cops will believe him."

The stand-by-your-man syndrome. Sam had called it right.

"What did Jack's dad think he should do?"

"Give himself up. I think he should, too, but he's

really afraid they'll railroad him just because he's been arrested a few times for smoking pot. I told him I'd get him the best lawyer money can buy, but he's scared, Caroline. We both are. I just don't know what to do.''

Caroline knew that if Becky got on that plane with Jack, she'd never see her alive again. Jack would find a way to get her inheritance transferred to his name and then he'd kill her. But if she tried to leave him now, he'd kill her that much sooner.

She wished Sam was here. He'd know what to say, what to do. But she had to make the call all by herself, and either way she called it, Becky lost the toss. It was just now—or later.

''I think Jack's right. Go with him, Becky, but I doubt you can get a flight out tonight. It's late.''

''We can. But it's—''

''You're leaving the country tonight?''

''No, I was wrong about that. There's no flight tonight. Uh…we're not leaving the country.''

She was lying. Jack had said or done something to make her change her story.

''I have to go, Caroline. But thanks. I knew I could count on you.''

Oh, yeah. Count on her to send her out of the country with a killer. What are friends for? ''Take care, Becky. Stay in touch.''

''I will.''

And that was it. Caroline dialed Sam's number, praying he wasn't on the phone or that for some reason he wasn't answering. Becky and Jack would be on a flight out of the country tonight unless Sam found a way to stop them.

He answered on the second ring.

THE PRENTICE PARK KILLER sat on his deck, which overlooked the offices of the *Prentice Times*. The apartment was old and dumpy, and the furnishings and curtains reeked of stale cigarette smoke.

Ah, but it was worth it for the view.

From his deck or his kitchen window, he could see if Caroline's car was in the parking lot. Sometimes he'd catch a glimpse of her when she came in or when she left. The view wasn't that great with his naked eye, but if he used the binoculars, he could see all her features. Her long, shapely legs. Her full breasts. Her seductive lips.

But he hadn't paid that much attention to her until that night in the park when she'd worn the red dress. He longed to see her in that again. And he would. He'd get her to wear that for him when they killed his next victim.

After that, they'd make love. She'd realize then that he was the one she should always have been with. But she'd made a mistake. Got mixed up with Sam Turner, which meant she'd have to die.

The plans were already made and falling perfectly into place. Destiny was at hand.

AFTER TALKING to Sam, Caroline went back to the file she'd been working on before Jack's call. Sam was going to run a check on every airport in Georgia, Alabama and nearby states, checking for late flights out of the country. And he'd alert the security officers at every airport to be on the lookout for Becky and Jack. He'd tried to assure Caroline that it would be virtually impossible for them to get through airport-security checkpoints and catch a flight out of the country tonight.

That should have made her feel a whole lot better. It hadn't. Jack had been standing there listening to everything Becky said. If he'd been planning to take a flight, he'd have changed the plans.

So what would he do?

Drive to Canada? Mexico? Those were long drives with a lot of chances to get spotted by cops along the way. So how could they get out of the country and not have to go through airport security? No way, not on a commercial airline.

"Yes!"

She called Sam back. "A chartered flight. They're leaving the country on a chartered flight. No security checkpoints. No passport required. Probably wouldn't even have to show ID if they flashed enough cash."

"Would Becky have that much on her?"

"I don't know. She might if they were in the process of eloping. If not, that diamond ring of her grandmother's she always wears would probably buy a small plane. And there are ATMs everywhere. She's filthy rich, Sam. That's why Jack chose her."

"You, my beautiful reporter, are a genius. I'll get back to you."

She prayed that would be soon. She went to the little kitchen at the end of the hall and started a fresh pot of coffee. She was high on adrenaline and still scared through and through, but she needed the caffeine to keep her alert and her reasoning sharp, in case Jack or Becky called again.

Jack Smith. He'd killed two women, then, afraid Trudy would connect him to the first victim, he tried to kill her, too. Caroline didn't know how the second victim fit in.

He might have been hitting on her, too. Or just stalking her and sending frightening notes. There was no way to know how many women he'd entangled in his web.

But then he'd met Becky, and her money had been too much temptation to resist. Friendly, trusting Becky who'd probably never had an enemy in her life.

"You're working late tonight."

"You scared me," she said, turning to find Ron standing in the doorway behind her. "I didn't hear you walk up."

"These quiet shoes," he said, lifting his right foot to show her the rubber sole. "What's up with the *Prentice Times*' prettiest reporter?"

"Careful. After the day I've had, flattery may get you anything."

"I doubt that, but I'll settle for a cup of that coffee you're brewing."

She was happy to share the coffee, but far too nervous to sit and make small talk. The minutes were ticking away and all she could think about was Becky.

"I talked to my friend today," Ron said, "the one who used to live at Meyers Bickham. I told him about you."

"What did you tell him?"

"That you'd lived there, too. That your mother

hadn't wanted you, either, that she'd just thrown you away with the morning trash.''

She really couldn't handle this conversation tonight. ''I'd love to stay and talk, Ron, but I'm really busy. I have an article I need to finish writing.''

''Did your detective friend find the guy who killed those two women?''

Her detective friend. Was there no part of her life that wasn't food for gossip around this office? ''No arrests yet.''

''Too bad. I hope they get him soon. If they don't, he's going to kill again. Men like that always do.''

And she definitely didn't want to think about that. She took her coffee and went back to her desk. She didn't write any more of the article. Her nerves were too ragged for her to think.

In fact, she'd had enough of the office. There was no reason to wait for Sam or one of his cop friends to pick her up. The killer was somewhere catching a plane. If she asked Ron, she was sure he'd give her a ride home.

She straightened her desk, stuffed a few things in her briefcase and was just about to go looking for Ron when Sam called with the good news.

''We got 'em.''

She sucked in a shaky breath. ''Is Becky all right?''

''A little hysterical, but unharmed.''

''Where were they?''

''At a small airstrip in the northern part of Georgia, almost to Chattanooga. They'd booked a charter flight to Cancun.''

The adrenaline rushed out of her and she went limp. "Thank God."

"And thanks to your quick thinking."

"You'd probably already thought of that, Sam. You're just too nice not to give me credit."

"We're a team. Detective and reporter."

"Who'd have ever thought that would happen? So is Jack in the hands of the police?"

"Both Becky and Jack are in the hands of the state police and on their way back to Prentice."

"But Becky's not under arrest?"

"No. She'll be released as soon at they get back to Prentice."

"Oh, Sam, I love you."

"Keep that thought until I see you."

"Will that be soon?"

"Not for a few hours. I've got some paperwork that has to be taken care of. And I want to be here when they bring Jack in so that I can be the one to book him."

"What about Becky's parents?"

"Becky will be calling them from the trooper's car. She'll probably call you, too."

"I can't wait to talk to her."

"Let me know when you're through at the newspaper and I'll have a patrolmen pick you up and give you a ride home."

"I'll be here late. I gotta get cracking. The biggest news story of my short career just broke."

"Not so fast."

"Now what?"

"We're officially only holding Jack for questioning at this point."

"And then what? You're not thinking of letting him go?"

"No. I can hold him for twenty-four hours without an arrest, then if I don't have enough evidence to arrest him on murder charges, I can jail him on a charge of attempted rape if Trudy will agree to press charges."

"I don't believe this. You know he's guilty."

"It's the way the system works, Caroline. I do one thing wrong, and the guy will walk on a technicality."

"Well, I don't like it."

"You change it then, babe. The pen is mightier than the sword."

Okay, so she couldn't write that they had a suspect in the murder cases. She could at least write that a suspect had been taken in for questioning. And nothing could dim her relief over the fact that Becky was safe.

And when Becky called a few minutes later, Caroline squealed in delight, so loud that the guys from the back who were getting ready to go to press came running out to see what was going on.

It was a celebration. Becky was safe and heading home.

IT WAS AN HOUR LATER when Caroline finished the article and took it to John. He read it over and for once had no suggestions on how she could make it better.

"Great job."

"Thanks."

"Has anyone seen Ron around?" she asked. "I was going to see if he'd give me a ride home."

"Take my car," John said. "I insist. Just leave it parked on the street in front of your house. I'll get one of the guys to drive me by there when we leave." He took his keys from his pocket, removed one from the ring and handed it to her. "Just punch the lock button when you get out and leave the key under the floor mat. It's the valet key. I still have the all-purpose one on the key ring."

"Sure you don't mind?"

"Not after the two weeks you've put in. Go home and get some rest. You deserve it."

ELAINE MITCHELL awoke and looked at the clock. It was 12:55 a.m. She'd been waking up at all hours ever since Trudy's accident, usually fighting to breathe. Tonight was different, thanks to the phone call she'd had a couple of hours ago from Detective Turner. The man who'd tried to kill Trudy was in custody. The nightmare was over. Her baby girl was safe.

Only her baby girl wasn't a baby. She was a very brave young woman. But it didn't seem that long ago when they'd brought her home from the hospital for the very first time. She'd been such a tiny thing, had weighed less than six pounds. Lots of new mothers had bouts of depression after their babies were born, but she never had.

Elaine and her husband, Brad, had tried to get pregnant for seven years before they'd finally been successful. Trudy was their miracle child. She still was.

The house was quiet. Brad was snoring away in the bed beside her. Trudy was safe in her own room just down the hall. She should go back to sleep, but she couldn't, not yet.

Moving quietly, she rolled out of bed and tiptoed down the hall the way she'd done every night when Trudy was little.

It had always made her feel better to stand in the doorway and watch Trudy's easy breathing as she slept. That steady rise and fall of her chest had been Elaine's reassurance that her baby girl was healthy and alive.

Tonight Trudy's door was closed. Elaine turned the knob and eased the door open. She didn't want to wake Trudy, but it was her first night home from the hospital and she should make sure Trudy was sleeping peacefully.

The bed was empty.

She almost screamed, but forced herself to maintain a semblance of control. Nothing was wrong. Trudy was in the house. She's gone to the bathroom. Or to get a snack from the kitchen. She might even be on the patio looking up at the stars the way she'd done the year she became fascinated with astronomy.

But even while Elaine's mind was forming safe scenarios, she was staring at the open window by Trudy's bed. When she flicked on the light, she saw the blood.

CAROLINE AWOKE to the sound of the doorbell. She looked at the clock. Ten minutes after one. It must be Sam, though she was surprised he hadn't just used the key she'd given him. She didn't bother to grab a robe, just crawled from between the sheets and padded down the hall in her bare feet.

She looked through the peephole, her hand already on the doorknob. But the man standing outside her door wasn't Sam.

What could Ron want at this time of the night—unless there was something wrong with John's car. Maybe she'd left the lights on and run the battery down. She just took it for granted that everyone's lights were automatic these days and operated on a delay system. She hadn't bothered to make certain they'd cut off.

"Hold on a minute," she called, then hurried back to the bedroom to get her robe. A minute later she released the safety chain and opened the door.

"Did I goof up?"

"Yes, you did, Caroline. Big time." Ron stepped inside.

"I left the key under the floor mat like John said."

"What?"

"The key to John's car. I left it under the floor mat, so I know that's not the problem. Is he having trouble getting the car started?"

"I'm not here about John's car."

Something in Ron's voice and the way he was staring at her sent a wave of apprehension zinging along her nerve endings. "If you're not here about the car, why are you here?"

"To see you. Were you expecting someone else? Someone like Sam Turner?"

His voice was accusing. Her apprehension became dread. This wasn't the nice, friendly guy she was used to talking to at the office. "Have you been drinking, Ron? Or smoking a joint?"

"A little of both."

"It's too late for you to be here. You need to go."

"But I'm not ready to leave. I was thinking you could put on that red dress you wore to my first party. I liked you in that. And wear those same shoes. They show off your legs."

The fear hit in waves now. She couldn't breathe. Couldn't think. Could barely speak. "It was you, wasn't it, Ron? You killed Sally Martin and Ruby Givens."

"I knew you'd understand about that, Caroline. We're alike, you and me. We were both there, with the rats and the people who punished you even when you tried to be good."

Meyers Bickham. He was talking about the orphanage. "So it wasn't your friend who lived there, it was you."

"Let's go get the red dress, Caroline. We need to hurry. Trudy is waiting for us."

No. This was all wrong. Jack was the killer, not Ron. And Trudy didn't even know Ron. She couldn't be with him.

"The dress, Caroline."

"You can't do this, Ron. I just talked to Sam," she lied. "He's on his way here."

"All the more reason to hurry."

She saw the gun then. Dark gray, a little bigger than his hand. She started to run toward the stairs, but he was too fast for her. He grabbed her arm and pulled her toward him.

She caught only a glimpse of the butt of the gun

as he came down with it, cracking it against her skull. And then she felt the warm gush of blood. The last words she heard were *red dress,* and then she started falling down the steep stairs, into the bottomless pit with the big gray rats.

Chapter Fifteen

Sam was already on his way to the Mitchell house when he took the call from the cop who'd been patrolling the area.

"That was fast," Sam said.

"I was only a couple of blocks away when I got the call."

"What's it look like?"

"An abduction."

"What did you find?"

"The bedroom window appears to have been jimmied from the outside. My guess is it was done with a crowbar, but that's just a prelim speculation. And there are fresh footprints going to the window and back again from a vacant lot next door."

"So the guy could have parked there and walked over."

"Yeah. Fresh tire tracks down the side of the lot closest to the Mitchells'. Vehicle probably bigger than a car. Could have been one of those vans or a light truck."

"May have to switch you to crime-scene details."

As Darkness Fell

"Any time. As long as I don't have to deal with the victim's families."

"I'm sure they're plenty upset."

"Mrs. Mitchell's hysterical. Her husband is livid. Says he'd turned the house alarm off when he went out to walk the dog. He didn't turn it on again after he got back. Blames it on you. Says you called and told them the guy threatening their daughter was in custody."

A mistake. Hopefully not fatal. But Jack Smith had admitted to running Trudy off the road. He was the one who'd threatened to kill her if she implicated him in the murders. With Jack in custody, she should have been safe.

"One other thing," the cop said.

"Shoot."

"There was only one set of footprints, but it looked like the guy might have carried something for a while, then dragged it the rest of the way."

"Something like à body."

"That would be my guess."

"I'm three minutes away."

"Then you're right behind Matt. He just walked in the front door."

Sam gunned the accelerator and took the next corner on two wheels. The Mitchells hadn't wanted a cop on duty at their house. Mr. Mitchell was a hunter with a houseful of shotguns, and he'd insisted he could take care of his own.

The department hadn't told him that they were staking out the house, anyway. The stakeout had been called off just two hours ago.

Until Sally Martin's murder, Prentice had been

such a peaceful town. The whole population couldn't have turned deadly overnight. Somehow Trudy's abduction was tied to the killer. A monster obsessed with Caroline.

Sam called the newspaper office. The phone rang a half-dozen times before a man answered. Sam identified himself and asked to speak to Caroline.

"She went home a little over an hour ago, Detective."

"How did she get there?"

"She took my car. I told her I'd pick it up later."

"Thanks. I'll call her at home."

He tried. After six long rings, the answering machine clicked on. Nothing to panic about. It was late. Caroline was probably asleep. But he couldn't let go of his uneasiness.

He called her again. She didn't answer. Sam spun the car into a U-turn. Matt would just have to handle things at the Mitchells' until he made sure Caroline was safe.

"I DON'T LIKE IT down here. It's scary," Daphne said.

Sara took her hand. "It's not scary. It's exciting. Like an adventure."

"As long as we don't get caught," Jessica said. "If we get caught out of our beds past lights-out, we're going to be in big trouble."

"What was that noise?"

"Probably a rat. They're everywhere down here. But they're as afraid of us as we are of them." Sara was always the brave one.

"Not as afraid as I am, I bet."

"We should talk them into letting us get a cat."

"Oh, sure, like they'd let us have a pet."

"I want to live with a family, instead of in this old ratty place," Daphne said. *"Then I could have a pet."*

"But if you moved in with a family, you couldn't be our best friend anymore, because you wouldn't be here."

"Oh, yeah."

"Let's play a game."

"What kind of game can we play with just a flashlight to see by?"

"Let's play I Wish."

"I wish I could go to Disney World," Jessica said. *"And live there in Cinderella's castle. I love magic."*

"But then you might have to kiss some creepy prince. Ugh!" Sara said.

They giggled. This really wasn't all that scary anymore, Daphne thought. It was fun. She liked having two best friends. *"I wish I had a house and a big family with grandmothers and aunts and uncles and cousins and lots of people to play with, just like some of those people on TV."*

"Wait a minute. I hear that noise again," Jessica said, *"and it is not a rat."*

"I hear it, too. It's coming out of that wall."

"It's a baby. A ghost baby."

No one was giggling now.

"Let's hold hands," Sara said. *"Hold on very tight in a circle. Ghosts can't break a circle of friends."*

They held hands, but the baby kept crying. And it didn't sound like a ghost at all.

"I think that's what happens if you're very bad,

like if you get caught down in the basement with your friends after lights-out. They just bury you in the wall, and you never come out.''

''I want to go to my room,'' Daphne said. ''I don't want to be buried in the wall.''

They held hands and walked back up the cold, dark stairs. And the baby in the wall just kept crying and crying and crying.

CAROLINE CAME TO slowly, dizzy and disoriented, her vision blurred. Strange memories played in her mind. She was young, playing with her friends in a cold, dark basement. She'd been asleep and this was the nightmare, but it had never been this clear before.

She tried to concentrate so that she could hold on to this part of her past when she woke up. Not the dark stairs, the cold basement or the heart-wrenching sound of a baby crying. But the good parts. Being with her friends.

''Won't be long now.''

Ron's voice cut through the thick fog that filled her mind, and she was aware of a whole new nightmare. She tried to sit up, but she couldn't move. Her hands were tied behind her back and her feet were tied together. The rope cut into her flesh. She was wearing the red dress. She didn't remember putting it on. In fact, the last thing she remembered was the crack of Ron's gun against her skull.

She must have blacked out. So Ron had dressed her. He'd touched her body. Her stomach churned at the thought.

But she couldn't give in to the fear or the revulsion. She had to use all her mental and physical energy to escape. So where was she? She looked around. Her vision wasn't as blurred now, but it was dark, and all she could see clearly was the back of Ron's head. And walls.

A truck. She was in the back of an enclosed truck, and from the way her body was being bounced around, they must be traveling at a high speed.

"Caroline."

Someone was in the truck with her. Or maybe she was sliding back into the nightmare—or just losing her mind.

"Caroline. It's me, Trudy."

"Either shut up back there or talk loud enough so I can hear you. I don't like whispering."

"Trudy Mitchell?"

"Yes. Who is that man, Caroline? Where is he taking us?"

"He works at the newspaper." And none of this made sense. "How did you get mixed up with him?" Caroline kept her voice low in spite of Ron's order.

"He broke into my bedroom while I was asleep," Trudy whispered. "He threatened me with a knife, told me he'd cut my throat if I made a sound. He did cut me a little. I felt the blood run down my neck and then he hit me in the back of the head with something that felt like a hammer."

"Probably the same gun he hit me with," Caroline whispered back.

"Probably. I woke up in the back of the truck. My hands and feet are tied."

"Mine, too." It still didn't add up. "Did you meet Ron at the Catfish Shack?"

"No. I've never seen him before, but he's going to kill me." Trudy started to cry.

"He won't kill you."

"Yes, he will. He told me so before he kidnapped you and threw you into the truck. He's going to kill me because he read what you wrote about me and he said I'm a lying slut. I'm not a slut. I'm not."

"No, and I never said you were. His mind is twisted, Trudy. Twisted and deranged."

Caroline had written about Trudy and Josephine's interactions. And she had notes on Trudy's testimony concerning Jack. But they'd never run in the newspaper. Nothing about Trudy had ever gone to print. Ron must have read the information about her directly from Caroline's computer late at night when no one was watching. Or else he'd read her private notes.

The Prentice Park Killer had been working at the *Prentice Times* all along.

And now he was in the white paneled truck that belonged to the newspaper. Normally it was used for delivering papers to the carriers and the dispensers located in various spots around Prentice. There was a barrier behind the driver to keep the stacks of newspapers from pouring into the front seat in the event of a sudden stop.

That was why all they could see was the back of Ron's head and the very top portion of the front windshield, and why it was all but pitch-dark in the back of the truck.

And now they were speeding down the highway—probably on their way to be killed the same way

Sally and Ruby had been killed. Throats slit. Stripped naked and left to bleed to death.

No. She couldn't think like that. She was a survivor. Sam had said so. She couldn't give up, especially now when she had so much to live for. For the first time in her life she loved someone who loved her back. Someone brave and strong and good. If only there was just some way to reach him and let him know where they were. Sam could stop Ron.

But Sam wasn't here. She had to do this on her own.

Her head pounded with pain, which became more excruciating with every bounce of her body against the floorboard of the truck. It was hard to breathe and difficult to swallow. She wet her dry lips with the tip of her tongue, then forced herself to interact with the monster.

"Where are you taking us, Ron?"

"To our place. Yours and mine. We were meant to be together, Daphne. You and me."

"And we are together. So why do you have me tied up in the back of the truck?"

"Because you screwed up everything when you started sleeping with Sam Turner."

She had to keep him talking, had to get a better handle on what this was all about. Then maybe she could find a way out. "I didn't want to sleep with him, Ron. He made me. It was you I wanted all along. Always you." The words gagged her, but she had to fight for life—hers and Trudy's. And she'd do whatever it took to stay alive until she was in Sam's arms again.

Whatever it took. The dread and revulsion swelled inside her and tears filled her eyes.

Oh, Sam. I love you so. I hope you know that. I hope you always know.

THE DOOR to Caroline's house was wide open when Sam arrived, and a table in the hall had been knocked over. Shards of glass from a broken vase were scattered about the floor.

Adrenaline rushed through Sam like water through an open floodgate. He rushed inside, searched every room, even the basement, where he knew Caroline would never willingly go.

The house was empty.

She was gone and he had no clue where to look for her. He stopped in the drawing room and stood in front of the fireplace, feeling as if someone had smashed a fist into his chest and ripped his heart from his body.

This is how it had been when he'd come home from work and found Peg's body sprawled across the floor, a bullet through her head. He'd never thought anything could hurt that way again.

He'd been wrong.

He'd known the other night when they'd talked about Peg that he cared deeply for Caroline. But he hadn't fully understood the depth of his feelings for her. But now, standing here in the drawing room where they'd made love that first night and knowing that Caroline was at the mercy of a madman, he realized he didn't want a life without her.

He had to find a way to get to her. The clues *were*

there; they always were. You just had to search until you found them.

Determined, he stormed into Caroline's office, turned on her computer and logged on to the Internet. He pulled up her e-mail and did a quick scan until he found the message from her stalker.

He read it slowly, though his heart was racing.

Hello, Daphne

I'm thinking of you, though I'm not happy you spent last night with Sam Turner. I had hoped you were saving yourself for me. But then, you don't really know me yet. You will soon. And you'll discover how very much we have in common. Much more than you have with Sam. He hasn't suffered as we have. But he will. Trust me, he will.

Take care, Daphne. Our destiny is upon us.

Sam printed the message and read it again.

This was their serial killer, not Jack Smith. Jack was mean and abusive, a pampered thug. But he wasn't in the same league as this guy. This guy was totally depraved, barely human.

Sam reread the message. Strange, but he felt drawn to the winding staircase, as if there was something up there he needed to know, or maybe it was just that he knew it was Caroline's favorite part of the house.

Taking the printed copy of the message with him, he climbed the stairs. He dropped onto the sofa, message in hand and tried to think what it might mean.

The guy was clearly upset because Caroline had

been with him. Not just that she'd been with another man, but that she'd been with him specifically—at least that was how it sounded.

But he spoke of something he and Caroline had in common. Was this guy a reporter? But how would that fit into the suffering? The suffering *they* had endured, but not Sam. And the guy seemed to take pleasure in calling her Daphne.

Sam looked up from the note and stared at the portrait of Frederick Lee Billingham. ''You've seen a lot go down during your years at the head of the stairs, Frederick. Lots of mothers giving birth, nurturing their children. Tell me what you know, good buddy. Steer me right. You're here every night. You gotta know how special Caroline is.''

Frederick stared down from the portrait and his eyes seemed to implore Sam to figure this out. Mothers who nurtured. They'd probably done that in this house. But that didn't happen everywhere. Caroline's mother had thrown her away like yesterday's garbage. Had this lunatic also been a orphan?

It was possible, even made sense in a way. At least it tied in with the shared suffering he talked about and with his calling her Daphne, which had been her name when she'd lived in an orphanage. They could have lived in the same one. Maybe that was the bond.

But obviously not at the Grace Girls' Home. Perhaps Meyers Bickham.

Meyers Bickham, the orphanage that had sprung straight from the bowels of hell. That was what R.J. had said about the place. He'd hated it with a passion and hated Sam because he'd lived in the home that

R.J. thought should have been his—miserable as it was.

R. J. Blocker. Out of jail on a technicality. A man with no conscience. Deranged enough to kill innocent people chosen randomly? Consumed with enough hate for the mother who'd deserted him that he'd take pleasure in killing innocent women? Evil to the core?

The answer to all the questions was a resounding yes.

Add to that the likelihood that the hate R.J. harbored for Sam would only have grown stronger while he'd been in prison.

The evidence and gut instinct both pointed to R.J. A combination that was almost never wrong.

Now R.J. had Caroline. Sam rushed out of the house with only one thing on his mind. He had to find the woman he loved before it was too late.

R.J. SLOWED THE TRUCK and pulled off the road, but on high ground so he wouldn't get stuck in the mud. The grass was high, and he didn't like high grass, was deathly afraid of the slimy creatures that slithered through it.

But he had to relieve himself, and it was safer to do it alongside the road than in a truck-stop rest room where someone might hear the two women call for help.

He took care of life's little necessity, then went to the truck and opened the back door. It always smelled of newsprint to him. And the black ink they used in the presses. He liked the smell of the ink.

He reached into the truck, grabbed hold of Caroline's arm and pulled her to the back edge of the vehicle. "I think it's time you and I got to know each other a little better."

CAROLINE HELD her breath as Ron tugged the top of her red dress down to reveal more of her breasts. She shook from a chill that seemed to harden to ice around her heart. She wanted to scream, to fight. But she was bound by rope. And screaming might make him kill both her and Trudy right now.

Her only hope was to close her mind so completely that she shut out Ron's touch, that she didn't feel his hands on her flesh. If she closed her mind, he couldn't reach her at all.

She tried, but still, revulsion nearly gagged her as Ron lifted the skirt of her dress and trailed his fingers up her legs. Her skin crawled as if he'd loosed a hundred spiders to parade across her flesh.

"You're beautiful, Daphne. And you were supposed to be mine."

"We hardly knew each other."

"We would have."

"We can still work it out, Ron, but first you'll have to let Trudy go."

"No. If you want me to believe you are with me now, you'll have to prove your loyalty, Daphne. You have to help me kill Trudy. I'll hold her, but you have to wield the knife. We can do it now. Kill her and leave her for the buzzards."

Trudy began to whimper.

Caroline shuddered. This was so sick, so horribly, horribly sick. Ron was completely insane. She didn't know how he'd managed to seem so normal at the newspaper day after day with such deranged thoughts and schemes in his head.

She had to think, had to buy time.

"We shouldn't waste that much time on her now, Ron. Someone might see us parked out here and catch us killing her. We should get out of here, but let me ride in front with you. That way we can talk and plan and get to know each other better."

"If you're sure you won't try anything…"

"I won't, I promise, but please untie me. The rope is cutting into my wrists and ankles."

Ron's face seemed to spasm for a minute, then he picked Caroline up and carried her to the passenger seat. Once he'd climbed behind the wheel, he reached under the seat and pulled out a hunting knife. Caroline's heart slammed against the walls of her chest as new waves of fear washed through her. But apparently he wasn't going to slit her throat just yet.

"Lean forward so I can get to your hands. But I'm leaving the rope around your ankles. And if you make any move I don't like, the rope goes back on the wrists."

She breathed a sigh of relief as the rope fell and her hands were freed. She'd passed the first hurdle. Her hands were untied and both she and Trudy were still alive. But now she was in the front of the truck, within reach of Ron's loathsome hands. She watched fearfully as he stuck the knife through his belt.

Thankfully, he didn't touch her again. He didn't even talk, just seemed to drift back into the madness of his mind.

Caroline concentrated on escape. She might be able to grab the wheel and make Ron crash the truck.

But that would only leave them stranded with him in the middle of nowhere.

She could hear Trudy crying softly. She wished she could tell her that she wasn't forsaking her and moving to the side of the enemy, but she didn't dare.

"Where are we going?" Caroline asked when Ron had driven about ten minutes without speaking a word.

"Home."

"This isn't the way to my house. You're going north."

"It used to be your home."

"Are you talking about Meyers Bickham?"

"Yeah."

"Why would we go there? You said it's a horrible place."

"Because Sam will go there looking for you. He has to be there when I kill you. That's what makes this whole thing so perfect. He didn't know I killed Peg, so her death was almost useless. But this time he'll know."

"You killed Peg?"

"Yes."

"Why?"

"Because Sam loved her."

He made it sound so mundane, as if killing a human was of no more consequence that swatting a mosquito. "Why do you hate Sam so much?"

"He stole my life."

"Did he arrest you for a crime?"

"Yes, but he stole my life long before that. While I was at Meyers Bickham, he was with my dad in a house with a yard and a bedroom of his own. A house without rats."

Oh, man, this was too crazy. But it added up. "You're R.J. You're Sam's stepbrother."

"Sam's no kin of mine. My dad just ran off with his slut mother."

"But why did you kill Sally and Ruby? Sam wasn't in love with them. He didn't even know them."

"Prentice is *his* town. He's supposed to be the hotshot detective, but no one thinks that of him now. Everyone with a TV or a newspaper knows that Sam Turner is a failure, just as I'd planned. No matter how he was raised, he's no better than me."

But Sam *was* better, a million times better, and she ached to feel his arms around her one more time before she died.

"You talk too much, Daphne, and I don't believe you, anyway. You're in love with Sam and that's just too damn bad." He slammed on the brakes and pulled the car onto the shoulder of the road. "I'm throwing you back with Trudy where you belong."

He jumped out of the truck and stamped in front of it, on his way to drag her from the front seat and throw her in the back. And in that second, Caroline saw her chance. She threw her bound feet over the gearshift and planted them on the accelerator, pushing as hard as she could. The truck jerked forward.

Ron was knocked onto the hood as the truck careened into a wooded area. He slipped off just as the truck came to a jolting stop against a large pine. Trudy screamed. Caroline went flying toward the windshield, but broke the force of the impact with her hands.

The engine sputtered and died, but a cloud of dark smoke billowed from beneath the bent and mangled hood. Caroline hadn't been seriously hurt, but she couldn't see where Ron was. Hopefully he was injured enough to slow him down.

"We have to get out, Trudy. Now!" Caroline tugged at the ropes on her ankles, but they didn't loosen.

"Did you kill him?"

"I don't know, but we have to get out and hide in the woods. And we have to hurry. The engine's on fire."

"I can't get out. I'm going to die," Trudy wailed. "Even if that man doesn't kill me, I'm going to burn to death in this truck."

"We're not going to die. I won't let us." But there were flames mixed with the smoke escaping from the hood now. They had minutes at the most. Maybe seconds.

Still, Caroline had to move with care. If she fell getting out of the truck, she'd have difficulty getting up again with her ankles bound. She might be able to roll to safety, but there would be no way for Trudy to open the back door of the truck.

She sucked in a deep breath of the smoky air, then slid to the ground. Her feet twisted, but she managed to fall against the truck and keep her balance.

"Come help me, Daphne."

Her heart raced even faster at the sound of Ron's voice. And then she turned and saw him, lying on the ground, his right leg bloody and crushed. He tried to get up, but he couldn't manage to do more than pull himself along in the high grass.

She turned away, nausea increasing, but she had to keep moving. Time was running out.

"You and me, we're soul mates, Daphne. You can't let me die."

"I can't help you, Ron. There's no time. And my feet are tied. I couldn't pull you away from the truck even if there was time."

"Then get my gun out of the truck so that I can kill myself before the car explodes."

But even if she could have done that, he wouldn't have shot himself, not until he'd killed her first.

She pressed her hands against the side of the truck to help her balance as she hopped toward the back of the vehicle. And all the while the flames coming from the hood shot higher. Sparks were catching in the wind, flying through the trees. All it would take was one colliding with the gas tank. One misplaced spark and they would all be dead.

Finally she made it to the back and was able to free the latch and lift the door. "Roll toward the door, Trudy. I'll help you out."

"I can't, Caroline. I can't move. The rope around my feet is caught on something."

"You have to work it free, Trudy. And you have to hurry." She couldn't keep the panic from her voice anymore. She didn't want to die.

"I can't get it loose. You have to help me." Trudy was crying, bordering on hysteria. "Please help me."

Caroline tried to jump into the truck, but she couldn't get any leverage with her feet tied. She could just fall to the ground and roll to safety now.

But if she did, she'd have to live with Trudy's screams for help ringing in her ears for the rest of her life.

She couldn't do it, couldn't leave Trudy to die alone. She fell to a heap and started tugging again, at the rope around her ankles. It seemed to take forever, but finally she worked the knot loose. Then she climbed on the back bumper and hoisted herself into the back of the paneled truck.

The rope that bound Trudy's ankles wasn't caught on anything. It was tied to a steel rod that was welded to the side wall of the truck. The smoke was so thick now that Caroline could barely breathe, but she kept struggling with the snarl of frayed rope. She needed the knife, but the cab of the truck was engulfed in flames now. The gas tank would go at any second.

The rope had been tied too tightly. It wasn't going to work free. Caroline crawled behind Trudy and linked her hands with Trudy's bound ones. "We have to hold hands," she said, choking on smoke and tears.

"How will that help?"

"I don't know. I only know that it does. Hold on tight and think pleasant thoughts."

"What are you thinking about?"

"I'm thinking that loving Sam Turner even for that short time has made my life worthwhile."

Chapter Sixteen

Sam had already called the state police and told them to drive to the old Meyers Bickham orphanage. He was driving there himself, sirens blaring, pedal to the metal.

He couldn't be certain that was where R.J. had taken Caroline, but it seemed a place R.J., with his twisted logic, would choose. And it was the only place Sam knew to try.

The road was dark. He'd hardly passed a soul in the last hour. But then it was already the wee hours of the morning.

It surprised him when he saw flames ahead. Maybe someone burning trash, though it was late for that. Or a stranded hitchhiker who'd built a fire to keep warm.

He was almost to it when he saw the truck with fire and smoke pouring from the engine. Damn. This was the last thing he needed tonight.

But there was no way he could drive by without making sure no one was trapped inside. He slammed on his brakes, barely controlling his own vehicle as he pulled to the shoulder, far enough in back of the truck that his car wouldn't catch on fire if the truck exploded.

It looked as though it might at any second. He'd have to be careful. No use risking his life if the occupants were out and safe. That's when he heard a woman crying, and it sounded as if it were coming from inside the truck. He took off running.

"Get out of that truck now! It's going to blow!"

"Sam."

He knew the voice. Relief and panic collided inside him as Caroline stuck her head out from the back of the burning truck.

"Get out and run," he screamed.

"I can't. Trudy's inside. She's tied to a railing and I can't get her free."

His feet flew the last few steps.

"Is that you, Sam?"

"R.J." Sam looked around, expecting to see his stepbrother standing there, pointing a gun at him.

"He's on the ground in front of the truck," Caroline said. "He's hurt bad. I don't think he can move."

"Then he can't hurt you." He lifted her out of the truck. "Run, Caroline! Get as far away from the truck as you can," Sam called, already leaping into the back of the truck. He took out his pocket knife and sawed through the gnarled rope. When Trudy's feet were free, he grabbed her and pulled her with him.

Caroline was still standing there, as if in shock. He reached for her hand and dragged both women to safety.

The gas tank blew before they'd gone a dozen feet.

They fell to the ground, Sam shielding Caroline's body with his as the sky rained fire and bits of metal and rubber.

When the explosion stilled, Sam cut the rope from Trudy's hands. They stood up slowly, one by one. Sam stood looking at the truck that had almost claimed their lives. The fire was still burning and the acrid smoke burned his eyes. R.J. had rolled to safety, but he wasn't going anywhere, not with the shape his leg was in. Nowhere except back to prison.

Sam pulled Caroline into the circle of his right arm. He reached out the other to Trudy, and together the three of them huddled in the fiery glow of chaos.

But all Sam felt was sweet relief and a passion for life he'd never known before.

"How did you find us, Sam?"

"R.J.'s computer message. And Frederick Lee Billingham."

He couldn't say more. His emotions were too raw. So he just held on to the woman he knew he'd love for the rest of his life.

Epilogue

Three months later

It was late May, the time of year when all of Georgia was perfumed with spring flowers and bathed in sunshine. The Billingham house was no different. Azaleas painted the lawn in shades of pinks and reds, and lilies cloaked in brilliant yellow nodded in the spring breeze.

A sprawling white tent, open on all sides, was set up in the backyard with a portable dance floor and tables topped with white linen cloths. A gleaming silver coffee server rested on one of the tables, a find from the Billingham basement, which Caroline had thoroughly raided over the last three months. And a four-piece band was already setting up in one corner of the tent for the late-afternoon wedding of Sam Turner and Caroline Kimberly.

"YOU LOOK absolutely beautiful," Becky said. "I'd like to hug you, but your dress is so exquisite and fragile-looking, I don't dare."

"The dress has been around for more than a hundred years. I don't think a hug from my maid of honor will destroy it.'' Caroline opened her arms and they embraced.

"You look happy," Becky said.

"I've never been so happy. I never dreamed I'd find someone like Sam."

"You deserve each other, and I mean that in the best possible way. You're living proof that no matter what the background, some people overcome it and turn into beautiful, decent people. And here I go getting all sappy when that's what you're supposed to be doing today."

"I'm sure I will. I just haven't gotten warmed up yet. But I know what you mean. I've thought about that a lot since the night we all came so close to death. Jack probably had everything he wanted growing up, but look how he turned out, compared to you."

"And you and R.J. both lived at least part of your lives in a frightful orphanage, but he wound up a vicious psychopath while you can't bear to even watch someone kill a bee."

"That was a honeybee you were swatting this morning. Honeybees perform a valuable service."

"See what I mean?"

"And then there's my Sam. He definitely didn't grow up in a nurturing family. But he's warm and loving and brave and strong and—"

Becky held up a hand to stop her. "Enough already. So, the guy walks on water."

"He is great. But I think everyone possesses the potential to be good or evil, and somewhere along the way, they make a decision that starts them down one path or the other. And if they just keep walking, they reach the destination—for good or for bad.''

''You sound so fatalistic.''

''No, and I don't mean it that way. I just mean that no one chooses what obstacles they encounter along the path, but everyone chooses their own destiny. R.J. chose his and tried to choose a destiny for me and for Sam, as well. But he forgot that we had choices, too.''

Becky stepped behind her, their two faces almost blending in the wavy mirror. ''I'm just thankful our paths crossed. And that you and Sam were there when I almost made a tragic mistake. I still shudder to think how taken in I was by Jack.''

Caroline turned at the sound of footsteps on the staircase.

''Hate to interrupt girl talk, but I'd like to talk to my beautiful bride for a few minutes before the wedding.''

Becky jumped in front of Caroline. ''You can't. It's bad luck for the groom to see the bride before the wedding.''

''Nothing about seeing Caroline is bad luck.''

Becky looked at the clock on the mantel. ''The 'Wedding March' starts playing in ten minutes.''

''Thanks for that update, maid of honor. Now why don't you run downstairs and make sure my best man is still breathing? Weddings make Matt extremely nervous.''

When Becky scurried off, Caroline turned to Sam. ''Hello, Detective,'' she said, sliding her arms around his neck. ''What's so urgent? And no quickies. We only have ten minutes.''

"I have a little something I want to give you before the wedding, Reporter Lady."

"A present?"

"Not exactly, because you'll probably have to pay for part of it." He reached into his breast pocket and pulled out a printed form and handed it to her.

She studied it for a moment. "It's a... Omigosh! This is a mortgage agreement for a house—for *this* house."

"You do want it, don't you?"

"Want it? Oh, Sam, I love this house!"

"Now it's ours."

"But the money. How will we pay for it?"

"We'll work and pay the mortgage. But don't look so frightened. The mortgage payment won't be any more than you were paying in rent. It seems that Barkley Billingham's grandmother has wanted to sell the house for years, but just couldn't find the right buyer."

"Probably because her grandson told everyone who looked at it that the house was haunted."

"Could be. At any rate, she only had one stipulation for the great price she's giving us. Frederick Lee has to maintain his place of honor until she's dead and buried. She wants no woe."

"I would never dream of removing Frederick Lee."

"I told her that."

"Oh, Sam, I love you. Kiss me."

"Okay, but don't start anything you can't finish quick. The 'Wedding March' starts in three minutes, and I don't want to miss a single beat."

Neither did Caroline.

Three minutes later she took her first step toward her groom, but just as she did, she caught a glimpse of the portrait hanging at the top of the stairs. She could have sworn that the stern-faced Frederick Lee winked.

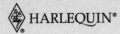

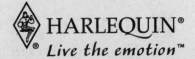

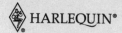

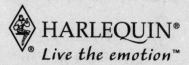

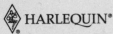

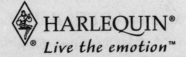

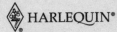

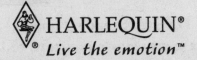